Untangled

A Spicy Holiday Novella

By Mallory Thomas

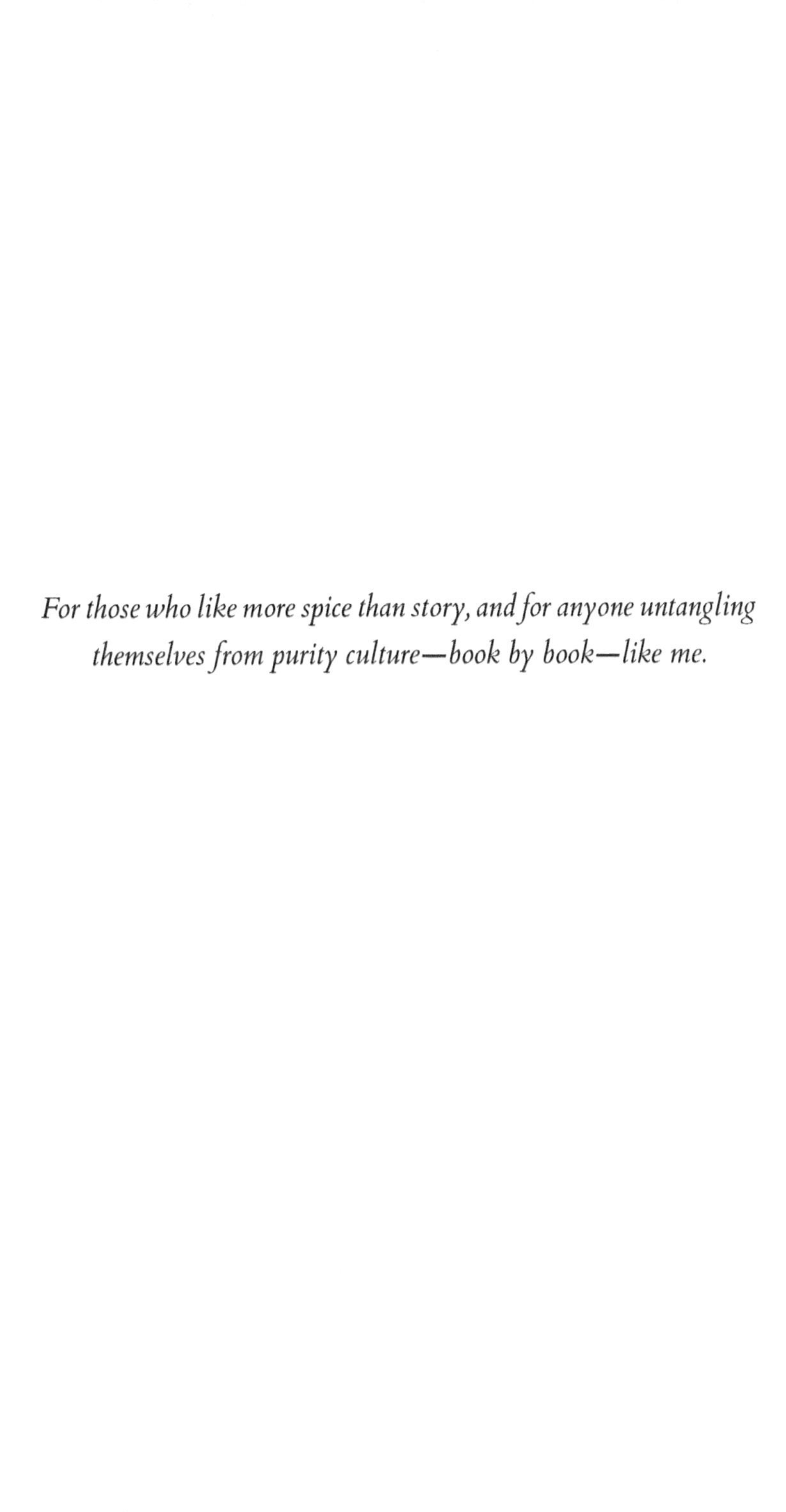

For those who like more spice than story, and for anyone untangling themselves from purity culture—book by book—like me.

Books by Mallory Thomas

Somewhere Along The Line

Untangled

Double Standard (releasing July 28, 2026)

Prologue

This isn't how I pictured it, being married.

Before you exchange vows, the folks in your life belong to one of three groups: friends, family, lover. When you take the person in the last category, whom you love most of all, and marry them? That whole category collapses. Two become one and three groups become two. Your lover turns family. Certainly, you don't *feel* about them the way you feel about your sister or grandfather, but even so, they join the family bucket. With this comes all of the benefits—security, unconditional love—and all of the consequences. Namely, such close proximity that no one knows you better. You know them with equal closeness, including that they leave their socks directly next to the hamper instead of *in* it. Their propensity to snore. The way they make the same joke whenever the opportunity arises.

What was once endearing becomes status quo.

And if distance makes the heart grow fonder, what about chronic exposure? What takes place in the heart then?

I promise, it's not all bad. Daniel is thoughtful. He asks me how he can help and follows through. He never complains about taking out the trash. He picks up dinner on the way home from work when I send an SOS text or a selfie with Violet's spit up in my hair. He's a great guy. So much better than the husbands of some of my friends.

But the whole thing—lifelong commitment—involves so little romance. Much more practicality, if I'm honest. Marriage is coordinating pest control and texting grocery lists and dropping passive aggressive hints about the division of labor. It's fighting over the right route to take to my parents' house and scrolling our phones next to each other on the couch and calling it "spending time together." It's eggs stuck to the bottom of the sink that someone didn't rinse down the drain.

Then you add in a baby, and the logistics multiply by ten. Your spouse is either a team member—the two of you passing like ships in the night, or rather, passing the baby—or an obstacle to your needs. The person you loved, that you still love, can feel more like a stranger than the lady that does your hair…if you had the time and the childcare to get your hair done these days.

And this continues until one day you wake up, eight years into marriage, feeling more like his roommate than his wife.

I feel more like his roommate than his wife.

It's this thought, coupled with a healthy dose of fear for what this means for the future, that has me adding the Amorous Advent card deck to my online cart at 1 a.m. on a Tuesday in late November.

24 Days To Rekindle Your Spark.

That's the tagline for a program with discussion questions and activities, one per day to complete with a partner.

We need something to get us out of this rut, because while he's a good man, and we have a good life, it's just so…uninspired.

Maybe we need just this.

Amorous Advent Daily Prompts

*A*uthor's Note: Read one chapter per day in the month of December, skip to the ones you want, or follow along with your own partner. If explicit sexual content isn't your thing, put the book down now!

1. What brings you to the Amorous Advent challenge? Share your hopes for the next 24 days

2. Discuss when you first saw each other, and what you

noticed

3. Hold hands while sharing what you'd like your life to look like ten years from now

4. Dance to your wedding song

5. Spend 90 seconds gazing into your partner's eyes

6. Give your partner a massage

7. What character trait do you appreciate most in your partner?

8. Kiss in your car (nothing further!)

9. Discuss your favorite past date, and how you'd modify it (if at all)

10. Have today's conversation naked—no touching each other!

11. Talk about the first time you said "I love you"

12. Explore what feels good to your partner using only your hands

13. What is your biggest pet peeve with your partner?

14. Explore what feels good to your partner using only your mouths

15. Celebrate with a night out together. You select what the other wears

16. What do you wish your partner knew about you, or your life together?

17. Share an intimate desire or sexual fantasy that your partner doesn't know

18. Try something adventurous you've never done

19. Discuss your favorite parts of your wedding day

20. Spend the day sexting

21. Praise your partner for their effort over the last three weeks

22. Connect outside the bedroom

23. Bake something together

24. Write a list of 10 prompts each to complete after the new year

Day 1

"Hey, babe?" I call to Daniel who has a bottle brush in one hand and a dish towel slung over his other shoulder. "When you're done, come in here; I have something to show you."

I debated all afternoon and evening about how to approach this, from the moment I got the small package addressed to Molly Hayes, confirming I did, in fact, commit to this challenge. *This challenge* being the card deck I hold in my hand, which I've decided (unbeknownst to my husband) holds the key to our future happiness.

Is that fair of me? To put so much pressure on a process my spouse doesn't know I've signed him up for? Probably not.

And yet.

I palm the deck in my hand, the stiff cardstock pressing against my fingers and leaving parallel dents across the tips. It's 7:30 p.m., the baby is down for the night and Daniel has, by the looks of it, two bottles left to wash. This should give me approximately one and a half minutes to decide the position I want to take here.

It's not that I think he'll balk; he is agreeable by nature, and this should—in theory—be fun. It's more that I worry he'll see this attempt to connect as an indictment of who he is as a husband, or evidence of my unhappiness with him. Just like a husband shouldn't buy his wife a vacuum for Mother's Day, perhaps a wife shouldn't buy her husband a pack of share-your-feelings cards, lest he think she believes he's emotionally stunted. I'll try to tread carefully.

"What's up?" he asks as he turns from the sink and strides into the living room. The street light streaming through the window couches his face in shadow and he looks softer, younger than he is. It's a flashback to Daniel at twenty-four when we were so certain about everything and didn't know we shouldn't have been. The moment is interrupted by a glimmer of light catching on the patch of gray hair that tufts from his widow's peak. He's thirty-two again as he steps toward me on the couch.

"Sit," I reply, while twisting my body toward his as he sinks into the leather. All six feet of him relaxes with a sigh—his arms stay loose at his sides, his legs fall open, he rolls his neck back and forth before rotating it in my direction. "So, I… have an idea for us," I say. "It's a little bit of work but I think it'll be worth it."

His eyebrows raise with curiosity. "Can I guess?" he asks.

I don't get a chance to answer before he starts.

"You're finally on board with us building a patio in the backyard?" His voice has a hopeful lilt that makes my stomach sink. I shake my head.

"Okay, maybe you want us to find and vet a babysitter so we can have standing date nights?" he asks. That *is* something we need to do, and the guilt of not being ready for it—leaving Violet with a stranger so we can do something as unimportant as eating dinner out—claws in my chest.

"No, it's not that. Though…" I sense an opportunity to connect the dots, and I take it. "It *is* about spending more quality time together. Want to see?" My heartbeat revs like the odometer on a Porsche that has seen a checkered flag. I hand Daniel the deck.

"A card game?" he asks. His chocolate eyes bounce between the stacked rectangle in his palm and my face, where I'm attempting to produce a casual smile.

"It's not a game, really. It's…more of an activity deck. There's a card for each day between now and Christmas, and we'll go through them together. Some have discussion prompts, others have tasks to complete. The goal is to, well, *rekindle* is the word they use. Find that spark again. I figured we could complete them in the evenings after Violet's bedtime?"

He makes a move to flip through the cards but I stop him with a hand on top of his. Even that unexpected bit of contact feels stilted, and if the simple act of laying my fingers on his skin is no longer easy or comfortable, we may need this experiment more than I thought.

"You can't look ahead," I say, catching his gaze. "The cards are in a specific order and build from one day to the next. If you're… if you're up for it, we should start with the first one."

My fingertips grip the edges of the deck and lift it from his palm. I take the cover card with its image of a gift box, a ribbon tied in the shape of a heart, and place it on the cool leather cushion between us. The next card, Day One, stares back at me. "Here," I say to Daniel and hold it for him to take.

"Hopes and goals?" he asks. He brings his other hand to his face and rubs it along his jaw. The stubble there scratches as it meets his skin.

"I know it's an unfair request because you haven't had much time to think about it, but maybe you could try? I'll go first," I offer.

While he hasn't officially agreed to this endeavor—for tonight or for the next several weeks—he also hasn't declined. I can only hope my vulnerability will convince him to share his own.

I steady myself with a deep breath that pushes my lungs against my pounding heart. "I miss who we used to be, *how* we used to be." Another deep inhale buys me time to collect the courage to continue. "Somehow, over the years, we've gotten so… knotted up in our roles and responsibilities, and then in being Mom and Dad, that it feels like I can hardly reach you anymore. My hope for this month is that we become…" I search for the right word. The silence stretches between us. "…untangled, I guess."

Daniel nods. He rakes the hand from his jaw through his hair, and the threads of silver catch more light as he does.

"I want that too," is what he says then. His eyes grow soft as he swallows. "Listen, I'm not sure how this works—the daily challenges or whatever—but I'd be lying if I didn't acknowledge there is…"

Now it's his turn to think, and I know he's searching for a turn of phrase that reflects our reality but doesn't condemn us. "There is room for improvement," he continues. "If you want to do this, let's do this."

"Yeah?" I ask. I didn't expect him to say no, but his easy agreement pinches my stomach. It's his implicit acknowledgement that things are strained enough between us to need something like this.

"Yeah. Maybe it will be fun," he says as his lips rise into a smirk. "Maybe I'll get to touch your boobs one day." He dodges left a split second before the pillow I intend to hit him with lands.

"Well maybe *I'll* get to share all the things you do that drive me insane, like how you take every opportunity you can to joke about my boobs." I say it with a soft smile, with a chuckle at the base of my throat.

"Molly, you know I take your chest very seriously." He levels his rich brown eyes at me and there's a playfulness that makes me wonder if the Advent cards could possibly work this quickly? "I would *never* joke about that."

I roll my eyes, slowly enough to really emphasize the point, and then lean over to nudge him in the shoulder. "Of course not," I reply. Turning my neck to hold his gaze, I ask earnestly, "You'll take this whole thing seriously?"

"I will. Promise."

With that, he reaches for the deck in my hand, slides the day one card to the bottom, and replaces the cover card on top.

"I will too. Promise, promise," I reply.

Day 2

Discuss when you first saw each other, and what you noticed.

The expectation of doing a new card tonight has had energy humming under my skin all day. It's not quite anticipatory jitters—the flutters in your belly before a first date, for example—nor common anxiety. It's something else entirely, a mix of fear and hope and curiosity swooping through my chest and squeezing around my heart. I've been counting down to 7:30 p.m. since Violet woke up a casual fourteen hours earlier and did not, to my dismay, go back to sleep. And now it's nearly here. Suddenly, I'm not sure I'm ready.

Daniel seems to feel no such nerves. He strolled in two hours ago, dropped his briefcase by the door, and was crouched low with open arms to greet our girl before I had a chance to say hi. God, how those two love each other. Sometimes I wonder if I'm the only mom in the world that feels like the third wheel in her family. If I always will.

No.

This is why the deck is important.

And with Violet tucked safely in her crib, lashes fanned across her cheeks, looking like the sweetest starfish in her sleep sack, I'm out of time for any lingering doubts about starting this experiment with Daniel in earnest. He knows it too.

"Ready, Molls?" He asks, finding me wiping the counter, newly clear after I've rehomed seventeen items that don't belong on the kitchen island. I turn toward him, and he looks like everything I don't feel. Calm, with a relaxed set in his jaw. Content, with a long exhale through soft lips. Easy, with the sleeves of his button down rolled to his elbows and an open bottle of beer in his hand. Handsome as ever, this husband of mine. Infuriatingly so, sometimes.

He takes a seat at the counter across from me, reaches for the Amorous Advent deck sitting next to the coasters, and slides it my way.

"Ready as I'll ever be," I reply, before discarding the cover and rotating the cards so we can read the one on top.

"Oh, this is simple," he says while drumming his fingers on the granite. "Want me to go first? I remember everything about the first time I saw you."

That night is clear to me too, wrapped in the warm glow of wistful nostalgia. I feel some of Daniel's calm start to loosen my shoulders, and I nod.

"That bar in Midtown," he starts. "Back then it was called Rock Bottom. Now it's something more trendy and up-tight—maybe The Loft? Doesn't matter. You were there with some friends, Lydia and Sara. You three were two bodies shy of a trivia team and Brett and I were the unlucky—*very* lucky, looking back—recruits you set your sights on."

At this, the warmth in my chest spreads. We were twenty three, barely dressed, and four shots deep when we spotted the boys. They didn't stand a chance. I shake my head but can't help the smile tugging at my lips.

He continues, "You were…this sounds corny, so bear with me, but I was hypnotized that night. I couldn't keep my eyes off of you. Your hair, blonder than it is now, was a mess of curls that you flipped one way and then the next with the beat. Long legs, black dress, bright blue eyes, plus a shock of pink on your lips. And you didn't know shit about a single category we were playing," he chuckles, and his eyes catch mine, "but your confidence never wavered. It was sexy as hell."

Admiration is the feeling that floods through me when I consider the woman he's describing. Can you admire yourself from afar, across years of distance when she—you—is no longer touchable? That version of Molly Hayes, or rather, Molly not-yet-married Hodges, feels like a mirage. Like something I conjured up to lure Daniel, who was looking for something me-shaped, before dissolving into the Molly I am now once he got close enough.

Sometimes I wonder who feels that loss more acutely—me or him. Sometimes I worry I'll feel parched for who I was for the rest of my life.

"That night was something, wasn't it?" he says, stealing my attention back to him and the way he runs his finger over the lip of his beer.

"*You* were something that night," I reply with an exhale that comes out like a huff.

"Was I?" he asks before raising the bottle to his lips and surprising me with a wink. It shoots straight to my belly, a low swooping sensation that's as unfamiliar to me now as Molly from eight years ago. It feels good though. Hopeful.

"Daniel, you were wearing a sweatband around your head and shouting out answers before the host even finished the questions. I'm pretty sure everyone in that bar was waiting for the bouncers to escort you out," I say with a laugh.

"Except for you?"

"Except for me. For some reason I still can't articulate, I found the whole thing endearing."

"It was the sweatband, wasn't it?"

"It was how you didn't take yourself so seriously. For as much as I projected self-confidence, I was super insecure. I wanted to look the right way, say the right things. But you—you joined our team and our table, and you were so unapologetic about who you were and what you were there for. Which, looking back, was getting drunk on vodka and feeling the full weight of glory from winning bar trivia," I say, and the memory takes on that fuzzy quality that comes with romanticized distance. "But also, you were tall. That helped."

"I'm still tall," he says, with a nod from across the counter.

"And you're still endearing," I reply.

Some of the time.

I catch the phrase before it leaves my mouth. Because the purpose of today's exercise, maybe of all of these exercises, is to focus on the positive.

"Some of the time," he answers anyway, and something that's been twisted tight behind my ribs releases at the unexpected moment of communion.

He knows what I know, which is that we're trying to learn how to love a different person than the one we fell in love with.

We have twenty-two days left to do it.

Day 3

*Hold hands while discussing what you'd like your life
to look like ten years from now.*

"That's it? Just talk while holding hands?" Daniel asks after pulling the day's card from the top of the deck. We're sitting on the couch again, the same cushion between us that might as well be the third party to our relationship.

"That's what it says," I reply, not wanting to question the methods of whatever couples therapist (*I hope it's a couples therapist?*) designed this experiment.

I feel tired today, worn down physically and emotionally, like the bones beneath my skin are unusually heavy. I'm not entirely sure why, but another early morning with Violet and Daniel's late arrival for dinner are part of it. I roll my shoulders to try and expel some of the tension that likes to hide itself there.

With the swish of his chinos against the leather, Daniel turns to face me, tucking one foot onto his opposite knee and holding out two open palms. In my head, I figured we'd sit side by side, my right hand in his left. He wants us facing each other, both hands held. It's a bid for more connection, and even in my weariness, I can appreciate the gesture.

I shift to mirror his position and place my palms on top. He rotates his hands beneath mine until he can separate my fingers with his and then fold them on top of my knuckles. He gives a gentle squeeze of encouragement.

"Look, we're already halfway done," he says, and it's a necessary bit of levity. It coaches a soft smile from my lips.

"A-plus effort so far," I say in reply. "Thanks for taking the lead on this one."

"You seemed like you could use a break. Want to talk about it?"

I consider it for a moment before deciding to use my current frustrations to inform my hopes for ten years from now. That seems like a more productive path forward. "I want to talk about the future," I say instead. "A decade from now—what do you see?"

"Well, to start, I'll be forty-two. That feels much too old, much too soon. Violet will be almost eleven. She'll probably be in full tween mode at that point. We need to figure out the parental controls on YouTube before then."

"I think assuming she'll want to watch YouTube on our living room tv, with us in proximity, is wishful thinking for eleven," I reply. The vision makes me happy nonetheless—a walking, talking, string-bean of a girl (if heredity has any say) with long blonde hair and her dad's chestnut eyes standing in this very room. Right now, at ten months old, she's much more of a squish than a person. It will be wild to watch that change.

"I'm sure my hair will be fully salt and pepper," Daniel adds, and the mental image expands to include him in the kitchen opening some mail. No more bottle rack next to the sink or high chair next to the table. There will have been days of small pink toys—maybe Barbies or bracelet making kits, things I can hardly conceptualize now—that are gone by then.

"You're supposed to be envisioning your dream life," I redirect with a laugh, "not ruminating on your age and hair."

"Okay fine, let me think," he says. His thumbs rub absent-mindedly across the thin flesh of my hands, and it's comfortable, sitting here with him like this. More so than I expected. "Ten years from now, huh. I want... I guess I just want to be happy. Hopefully I'll be a managing partner by then. I want to come home to this house, to you and Violet. Maybe another one? A little sister or brother. I want to support them in whatever sport or activity or interest they have and feel like the proudest dad in the world. Maybe we could travel since the kids will be older. I'd love to go to Europe with you. Or if not, maybe we could spend our evenings on the back patio we finally built."

At this, I level him with a look.

"What?" he replies, with a tone just north of teasing and another small pulse against my hands. "This is *my* ten year plan. I can include whatever I want, same as you. But seriously, though, I just hope we're all healthy and happy. That's the big dream."

"That's my big dream too. Healthy and happy and thriving." I think for another moment, squinting my eyes as though that may help me see the future clearly. "Maybe another baby, although that threatens the 'thriving' part for me, at least for a while."

It's a statement we both know is true. My pregnancy and postpartum with Violet was rough to say the least. "But maybe by then, ten years from now," I continue, "I'll be far enough removed. I'd like to be working a job I really enjoy, with the kid—kids?—in school. Something hands on that doesn't have me stuck behind a computer all day. I'd *really* like for both of us to arrive home each evening for family dinner, to be done with never knowing when you'll wrap up for the day."

He nods, and his eyes search mine, maybe looking for that frustration or exhaustion I felt earlier. I don't feel it so acutely now.

"Most of all, though, I'd like to sleep," I say on a laugh. "Do you think that's doable?"

"God, I hope so," he replies, before silence stretches between us.

"Ten years from now," I interject. "Wow. It sounds like a good plan."

"It'll be here before we know it."

"Yeah. Now we just have to figure out the plan for getting there," I reply.

"You know, I think these nightly activities are a good start."

Day 4

Dance to your wedding song.

Violet sits at the head of the table, banging a spoon on her tray and using the other hand to press roasted sweet potato into a paste. Streaks of orange pop on her wispy blonde hair where she's taken to patting her head. She babbles to Daniel as he makes a silly face, and the scene is typical for a weeknight dinner in the Hayes household.

Thinking back to our conversation yesterday, about our lives ten years from now, I'm preemptively nostalgic for this moment in front of me. Daniel is right—it's going to disappear too soon. I try to memorize Violet's chubby hands with the dimples over her knuckles and the way she giggles when I wiggle my eyebrows at her. I look over at the man who shares her eyes and the cowlick at her forehead and yes, maybe we aren't as close as we once were, but I'm lucky he's mine. I do feel that way, on a conceptual level. While we lack the magnetism of when we first got together, that was the result of hormones and brain waves. What we've built since is from years of choosing each other, and that has to mean something.

"Excited for tonight's card?" he asks, turning to me before lifting his fork to his mouth. "So far it's been a lot of talking and not a lot of…activity. I wonder when that's going to change."

"We're less than twenty percent in," I reply. "I've gotta assume they save the good stuff for the second half."

"The good stuff, eh? You sure we can't peek ahead?" With this, he raises one eyebrow and pulls his bottom lip between his teeth.

I need to be clear: we have sex. We had this baby, after all, and we've been intimate since with some regularity. This is not a man deprived. Maybe it feels a bit rote, sort of… compulsory, but I'm holding up my end of the bargain. The implication that he wants more, with that raised eyebrow, turns the air between us taut. What was just soft with appreciation feels sharp.

"Yeah, that's a no. We're following the plan as written, but nice try," I say.

"Worth a shot," he replies, before turning back to his plate and reengaging with Violet.

I push back from the table and grab the deck of cards from the island. What does Day 4 say? If I was wrong in my assessment and it *is* something sexual this early in the process, I need to prepare myself. I slide the day's card from the stack and look it over.

Dance to your wedding song.

Physical? Yes. Sexual? Not particularly, which is a relief.

"Looks like we're dancing tonight," I say to Daniel as I sink back into my seat. I toss the card his way and he catches it under his palm.

He nods and squints like he's trying to recall the memory of our first dance, to place the title and artist.

"It's Ed Sheeran, *Thinking Out Loud.* A top hit of the mid 2010s, if that's what you're wondering."

"I know," he replies. "I was trying to remember the tune."

Grabbing my phone from the chair beside me, I find the song in my library and press play. There's only one chord before the lyrics start, and the song is blissfully simple in its orchestration, directing all attention to the words. We listen in silence, save for Violet's occasional trills, and the phrase about falling hard at twenty-three knocks the breath out of my lungs. We lived that part. Can we live the rest?

"What if we dance now?" Daniel's interruption surprises me.

"You don't want to wait til she's down?" I ask, nodding at our sweet girl who, based on the volume of food on the floor, seems to be done with her dinner.

"We could, if you want. But we could also dance with Violet. Make it a family affair."

That sounds nice. Easy. Less potential for awkwardness than the two of us fumbling over our feet and words after his comment earlier fell flat.

I nod, grab the packet of baby wipes—the centerpiece of our table in this season—and get to work cleaning up. Violet protests, flails, pushes me away and it's like trying to restrain a feral raccoon every time I wipe her face. Daniel plucks her from her chair, sets her on his hip and tilts her back and forth, prompting delighted squeals. He extends his free hand to me and I reset the song to the beginning.

With my arm around his waist, he drapes his over my shoulder. It makes for a weird sort of line with Daniel at the center and his girls on either side. I bring my other hand to wrap around Violet, my arm resting on top of his, to make us into a circle. Bringing my cheek to his chest, I let myself lean into him. He's solid, though a bit softer on top of the muscle than he used to be. My head fits where it always has, in the divot under his collarbone. I nuzzle against the soft flannel of his shirt and a contented sigh, so quiet I'd have missed it if I wasn't right here, leaves his mouth and blows warm against the skin of my neck. Goosebumps spring up where it touched.

We continue to sway, and Violet snuggles into Daniel further. My eyes catch on hers and they're heavy from the movement and the late hour. The fight from before has left her little body, and she's calm, noodle-boned. *This is her home,* I think. Not just this house and this room, but Daniel's arms. My eyes. The warmth of this moment. I feel lucky again.

The song loops to the beginning and we don't stop dancing. The heavy weight of Daniel's hand comes to rest at the back of my head, his forearm between my shoulders radiating warmth across my back. He tucks me against him until we're nearly flush, minus Violet between us on one side. His fingers thread through my hair and scratch against my scalp. Up and down they run, pushing at the skin and then dragging down with the scrape of his fingernails. It's *heavenly.* My resulting "mmm" sounds more like a moan than I intend. My quiet "thank you" is breathier than it should be. But it feels so nice to be touched with tenderness like this. Without the expectation to rush to "the good stuff." I want more of it.

Want.

I barely recognize it at first, building low and slow in my stomach. God, how long has it been since I've *wanted* his touch? I'd like to analyze this, stew on it, and probably berate myself for it but the firm press of his hand, the familiar smell of the detergent he likes—that I know he likes—brings me back to the moment. The weight of him growing hard against me is unexpected, but it doesn't feel like a threat. It feels like a reply to the question that led us here: *Are the two young fools who fell in love still in there somewhere, and can we find them again?*

Tonight, I wonder if the answer could be yes.

Day 5

Spend 90 seconds gazing into your partner's eyes.

We didn't have sex last night. After the song ended for a third time, Violet was asleep. I slipped from Daniel's side and watched as he tip-toed into her room and placed her in the crib with the precision of someone handling a live grenade. He snuck out after transferring her successfully and we just…looked at each other for a while in the hall. I'm not sure either of us knew what to make of our experience dancing in the dining room. Talking about it felt like it might break the spell, and it didn't make sense to start up the song again. The moment had passed, idyllic as it was.

Then it was back to our regularly scheduled programming: both of us rotting on the couch. He watched sports highlights on the ESPN app, I scrolled TikTok and bookmarked recipes I will undoubtedly never make. We traded thoughts here and there, and then went to bed, rolled to face opposite walls, and passed out.

Now it's evening again, and we don't have Violet to act as a buffer as we stare down the barrel of another card. My hands prickle with nervous energy as I wait for Daniel to change out of his work clothes and join me in bed. Yes, we decided to do this one in bed; TBD on whether this was a good or bad idea on my part.

I palm the deck in my hands and resist the urge to peek at today's prompt. I told him I wouldn't, that I would wait so we could read it together, and I will. Squeezing the cardstock and tugging on the soft weight of the comforter to straighten it keeps me occupied until I hear his closet door open. He shuffles into the bedroom on socked feet sliding across the hardwood. The same college t-shirt he's had for ten years, maybe longer, stretches across his shoulders, though it's lost elasticity in the collar over time. He lifts the covers on his side of the bed and slides underneath, sitting to rest his back against the headboard.

"Let's see what comes after dancing," he says, nodding to the cards in my hand.

"I didn't peek!" I reply, wanting him to be as proud as I am at my self control.

"Good girl," he says, and *wow* if that doesn't light up every one of my nerve endings without my consent. I'm immediately overheating and digging my legs out from under the comforter to place them on top. Has he ever said that to me before? I don't think so. Maybe in passing.

Definitely never in bed.

Hmm.

I flip the card in his direction and wait for him to read it to me.

He doesn't read it out loud. Instead, he says, "Alright, set a timer on your phone for ninety seconds."

"For what?" I finally ask, after letting his request hover between us for about that long.

He passes the card to me and I scan it. Ninety seconds isn't a lot. This might be the easiest prompt yet.

When I've got my phone in hand, I swipe the screen to bring the timer to one and a half minutes. Like we did on the couch, Daniel turns to face me and I twist my body to mirror him, drawing my legs up to cross them. The phone sits on the covers between us.

"So, is this a staring contest or what?" I ask, trying to bring a little levity to an activity that feels strange, if straightforward.

"Pretty sure you're allowed to blink," he replies, before leaning over and pressing start.

My immediate thought is: we should've cued up some music.

My next thought is: I was wrong. Ninety seconds will feel like a long time.

Daniel's eyes hold mine as the seconds, presumably, start to pass. I don't dare look down to check out our progress. Instead, I really *look* at him.

Of course, I know what he looks like. I could pick him out of a line-up based on any one of several individual facial features. I see him every day, in many different contexts, and have for nearly a decade. I know this man's face as well as I know my own.

And still.

Looking at him like this feels different. I catalog the growing collection of creases that feather out from his eyes. The richness of the brown there, almost indistinguishable from the dark depth of his pupils. An age spot on his cheek, next to freckles he's had for longer than I've known him.

He clears his throat and I think about what he sees with me. The wrinkles that line my forehead, new in the last few years? The hollow half-moons under my eyes from disrupted sleep? The way my neck is starting to sag, no matter how much tightening cream I use in an attempt to combat gravity?

How many seconds has it been?

I drag my attention back to his face, to his eyes that shift ever so slightly back and forth as they take me in. The eyes that grew damp and red on our wedding day and then large with shock when I told him about the pregnancy. The same ones that appraised me all those years ago at trivia and deemed me worthy of his attention, and later, his affection.

Beep! Beep!

The sound of the timer snaps me back to a reality where I'm sitting on my bed and feeling remarkably exposed.

Daniel brings a hand to rub down his face, like he needs a moment to shake off the experience too.

"Any reflections?" I ask, unsure where we go from here. I wish the card had provided some wrap-up instructions.

"It was really nice to just…be here with you," he replies. "I think I like these activities. I'm excited to do them with you every night."

"Yeah?"

"Yeah. I get so caught up in what needs to be done, distracted with work, making sure all the pieces fit there and at home that sometimes I'm on autopilot. Doing something different like this, it's been good for me. Hopefully for you too."

"Agreed. I may not understand the methodology—and don't get me wrong, your eyes *are* very handsome—but maybe it's less about the task and more about the daily commitment to spend time and effort on each other. On us."

He nods before snagging one of my hands and asking, "You know what I was thinking during the staring contest?"

The phrasing makes me chuckle. "Hmm, that becoming a mother has aged me for the worse?"

"No. Absolutely not. I was thinking that if I had known you were going to look this good in your 30s, I would've locked you down sooner."

"You did not," I add with a scowl, resisting the urge to roll my eyes.

"I did, and I stand by it." His tone is as sincere as I've ever heard it. "Listen," he continues, "I don't tell you enough how grateful I am for you. I know I haven't been the most available, emotionally or otherwise, in too long. I know I'm not as flexible or attentive as you deserve, and I've left a lot of apologies unsaid. I've been thinking over the past few days about how we got here—why you wanted to do this with me—and I want to own my part of it. Thank you for bringing me the opportunity to do that."

I…

Bowled over, is how I feel.

Some combination of surprised and pleased and grateful mixed with disbelief.

Daniel has never been the most expressive. He waited a year to tell me he loved me, though it was obvious eight months earlier, to both of us. So hearing him wrap up these thoughts and hand them to me without reservation is a gift bigger than he knows.

"No, thank you," is the only way I can respond. "Thank you for saying that."

He leans over and presses his mouth to mine, the ritual of a goodnight kiss we've kept through the highs and lows of the last eight years. But today it feels different, charged with new energy. It's familiar, comfortably so, but with a little something extra, like a twist of lime in a favorite drink. Heightened. It lasts for a second longer than normal before he pulls away.

"I mean it, Molly. I really do."

Day 6

Give your partner a massage.

His fingers spread wide over my shoulder blades and push into the muscle at the base of my neck. They are deliciously warm. He intended as much when he rubbed his palms together to generate heat, a byproduct of friction.

It's funny, isn't it? But true:

So often, we butt heads. We grate against each other. It builds into simmering frustration that sometimes, inexplicably, becomes sexual tension that spills over.

Friction, then heat. The first law of thermodynamics *and* the working principle behind make-up sex.

Friction. The word may be gentler than what's accurate to describe the state of affairs between Daniel and I.

I needed two things from him today: to pick up eczema cream on his way home from work, and to get his golf bag out of the front hall. I have a crystal clear image of holding Violet on my hip, balancing a diaper bag on one shoulder with the car seat hanging from my opposite hand, a few pieces of mail stuffed between my teeth because I'm out of available fingers, and then launching Violet headfirst toward the floor when I slip on the golf towel hanging from the side of his clubs. The police would investigate us for abuse when I take her to the hospital for a skull fracture, not knowing the real crime would be the plot against my husband I'd undoubtedly be crafting.

I told him yesterday about both requests: the cream and the clubs. I asked for five minutes of his time to ease my nerves. To save me the effort of going to the store, since he could run in without having to unbuckle and rebuckle the baby.

Now it's 7:30pm and neither thing happened. He'll get to it tomorrow, I'm sure. But every time I attempt to squeeze the last rations of cream onto my fingers for Violet's scaly legs or see the green-smeared sides of his golf shoes on the floor, I'm filled with unbridled rage. They might as well be screaming at me, "I hear your needs and I don't care." Maybe, "My time is worth more than yours." Like I said, rage.

As such, dinner was silent. Even Violent seemed to get the hint, and Daniel brought her to bed without my prompting or instructions. With tension thick in the air, I wondered if tonight might be the first night we skip the day's card.

Instead, he caught me in the bathroom brushing my teeth, already wearing my pjs, and suggested we keep the commitment. He'd be waiting on the couch, he said. *Take your time.*

And now we're here, that same silence crackling around us but now with his hands on my skin as he sits behind me. Words don't seem to be working, so maybe we can communicate this way.

He takes a thumb and presses it along the ridge of my spine, kneading slow circles with increasing pressure, trying to get the muscle to soften. When he's pleased with the effort, he moves down a vertebra and continues the pattern.

The slow drag of his thumb is remarkably intimate. The splay of his palm between my shoulders prompts a shiver, a memory of him pressing right there as he holds me against the mattress, my knees hiked up and legs open for him to enter me from behind. The weight of that hand grounding me, when my body was his and my mind was outside its usual confines.

I shiver again.

"You cold?" he asks as he continues working my back.

"Not really," I reply, but it would be more convincing if the thin fabric of my tank didn't show my nipples at attention.

Without further discussion, Daniel peels off his hoodie and, after sweeping my hair to one side with a brush of fingertips against my neck, places it over my head. I thread my arms through the sleeves.

"Better?" He asks.

"Warmer," I reply. Because is it better? This sweatshirt smells like him and feels like home. How does one stay angry when confronted with tactile memories and wrapped in fleece? Maybe that was his goal all along. I can't help but question, "But aren't you cold now?"

"Nah, I'm fine."

"Are *we* fine?" I ask.

He pushes air from his nose, the barest hint of a laugh within the huff. "You tell me, Molls. You seem upset."

"I wonder why," I reply, with more petulance than necessary.

"I'm not a mind reader, babe. I can't meet your expectations if you haven't shared them."

"I did share them! I told you what I needed! I'm *always* going on about this, Dan. We've had this conversation fifteen times."

"About the chores? Like I've said, I can do more if you make me a list. I'm happy to help."

"It's not about chores!" I say, louder than I should with a sleeping baby down the hall. The volume startles Daniel's hands from my body. I turn to face him. "I don't need your *help*. Help implies that you're doing me a favor. You live here and are an equal member of this household. I need you to *see what needs to be done*, Dan. Making you a list is another job on my plate. Take a look around, use your eyes, and then act. I want to be your partner, not your manager. Not your mother."

It's a low blow, a petty but intentional push against the hurt of his poor relationship with his parents, for whom he's never been good enough. I regret it as soon as I say it, because the unspoken part landed loud and oppressive: you're not good enough for me either.

"Sorry, that's not, I didn't..." I scramble to say.

"Don't say you didn't mean it."

"I shouldn't have said it."

With a furrowed brow and downcast eyes, Daniel slips from behind me to sit at my side. The silence hangs in the air like a storm cloud, dark and heavy.

"Whether or not you should've said it, you *feel* it," he says, "and God, if that isn't worse. I'm really trying, Molls. I don't want to let you down. I'm trying to be there for you and be attentive to work and be present for Violet, and I'm pretty sure I'm failing at two of the three every day. What they say about dropping balls—about making sure the ones you drop are plastic and not glass? In my head, rash cream is plastic. My golf bag is plastic. What's one more day, so I can keep the important stuff in the air, you know?"

"But that's..." A stinging pressure builds behind my nose, starts to bind in my throat. I breathe in deeply before I continue. "If the important stuff is in the air, and the stuff I need from you is not, then my needs don't feel important to you. That's what I'm trying to say."

"Molly, no. Shit. I'm so sorry." He scrunches his face tightly before releasing it with a blink. "I understand why you might feel like that, but it's not true. You're more important than anything else," he replies, grabbing my hand and linking his fingers with mine.

"Then make me feel like it. Please, even if what I'm asking from you seems small or silly, spend the time and follow through. That's the best way you can love me, and the best way I can trust you."

"I want you to trust me. And I know I won't always get it right, but I can do better. Let me get my stuff out of the front hall now and then I'll run the store. I'm sorry," he says.

"How about you clean up your golf stuff, and *I'll* go to the store. I haven't been out of the house all day and could use the break. Thank you. For listening to me and trying to do better and for not acting like I'm crazy."

"You're not crazy. You're holding our family together and dealing with my shit on top of it. Thank you for telling me." He leans in to kiss me and there's a promise in the tender brush of his lips against mine.

"Now go sit in your car and scroll or listen to music or drive through McDonalds for a milkshake on the way to the store," he says. "Whatever you want to do. When you get back, the entry will be clear."

"Thanks. And we'll do a rain check on the massage," I say as I stand up from the couch and smooth my hands over my thighs. "Next time I'll start with you."

"You'll have to fight me on that," he replies as he makes his way to the front hall, eyebrows raised.

"I'll give in then. No more fighting."

"No more fighting," he says with a nod. "I can get behind that."

Day 7

What character trait do you appreciate most in your partner?

"What can I get you to drink?"

The waiter, who doesn't look a day over twenty-two, waits expectantly for my order with a small pad of paper clutched to his chest. He flicks his head to fling dark hair from over one eye.

"I'll have a glass of the house white," I reply before turning my eyes to Daniel. Now we both wait while he peruses the drink menu, humming softly while he does. Even though he's taking his time looking everything over, he will, without question, order an Old Fashioned.

"Hmm," he says, right on cue. "I'll take an Old Fashioned. Do you have Blanton's?"

"We do. I'll get those right out," the waiter says, while not writing anything down on that notepad of his.

My *thank you* trails off as he leaves the table before I've said the second word.

"This is wild, huh?" Daniel says as I turn back to face him. We're sitting at a two-top, tucked against a window. The soft edge of the tablecloth tickles my bare knees every time I cross them.

"Eating dinner? That's pretty typical across cultures," I joke.

"Going to a nice restaurant. It's been almost a year, I think."

"Since before Violet," I add.

After the mess that was yesterday's fight/massage, I sent a frantic text to my mom asking if she could watch Violet tonight. I figured the change of scene could help both of us re-center. I didn't anticipate that being away from her would spin up my nervous system just as much as being with her. While the restaurant protects me from the constant sensory overload I feel at home, it's a struggle to keep my mind from straying with worry.

"Are you thinking about Lettie?" Daniel asks and I nod. "Me too. I always thought it was weird when parents would say they spent time away from their kids looking at photos of them, but now I get it."

"Do you think my mom is going to remember the extra pacis when it's bedtime?"

"You laid everything out for her. And she raised two kids of her own—she's not new at this."

"A lot of what they did back in the late 80s and early 90s is illegal now. That's not the comfort you think it should be," I say.

A different server appears, with curly hair in a bouncy ponytail and a few wisps pulled out on the sides. She drops our drinks on the table with a quick, "Enjoy."

"Should we toast?" Daniel asks.

"To what?"

"Hmm, to prioritizing ourselves, to the advent challenge, or to your mom. You pick."

"To enjoying a night off," I say instead, before tilting my glass for him to clink.

"Hear, hear," he replies.

Quickly, my mind drifts back to Violet and whether the diaper I placed on her changing table, along with her pjs, was the more absorbent night-time version.

"She'll be fine, Molls. Ready for today's card?"

"Hmm?" I shake myself out of my questioning to Daniel drumming his fingertips on the deck, which he's placed on the table.

"Want to read today's prompt?"

"Oh, yeah, sure," I answer. "Let's hope it's appropriate for public discussion." So far, none of the prompts have been particularly risque, much to Daniel's disappointment. With today marking the end of the first week, I wonder if that's about to change.

"What character trait do you appreciate most in your partner?" he reads, before flipping the card back and forth between his pointer and middle fingers.

I breathe a sigh of relief that it didn't ask us to discuss our favorite sex positions. *This*, I can do here. He smiles, soft and genuine.

"You're going to get a big head, aren't you?" I reply, lifting my eyebrows in his direction.

"Depends. How nice are you going to be?"

"You can grade me on it when I'm done," I ask, before pulling my lips between my teeth to think. "Hmm, favorite character trait. If it was a physical trait, the answer would be obvious: your hair."

"That's obvious?"

"Yes! I love your hair. Also your shoulders, but that's another conversation for another time."

"Or we can continue it now…" he says, taking a sip of his liquor.

"No, I can answer. My favorite character trait is that you're loyal. Actually, how about the top two? Loyal and level-headed. You'd die for me and Violet— literally. If a bus were coming our way, you'd jump in front of it and try to stop it with your bare hands. If a woman approached you at a bar, you'd show off your wedding ring and tell her what an amazing wife I am. And when I'm catastrophizing—like right now, with Violet at home—you speak to my heart with logic and assurance. You always know just when I need it."

His face softens with the words, melts into a calm, content expression while his eyes spark with pride.

"That's exactly what I want to be for you. Thank you for saying that. I'll try not to let it go to my head but that was quite the compliment, so no promises," he replies with one side of his lips turned up, devious. I kick him gently under the table in response.

"My turn," he continues, without acknowledgement of my wandering foot. "You are so patient, Molls. I watch you with Violet and you have the patience of a saint. You let her figure things out herself when my hands are screaming to *just fix it, already*. You are patient with me too, with the ways I fall short and with my stupid dad jokes and when I get home late for dinner. And you're curious too. You genuinely want to know how people are doing, and how you might help them. You want to find solutions—like this Advent challenge you found for us. Your curiosity is one of my favorite things about you."

Well, if it isn't my heart swelling two sizes in my chest, like the Grinch himself, under Daniel's praise. God, I want to pluck this feeling and place it in a jar, beautiful and delicate, to store behind my mirror for the days when all I see in myself is failure.

"How's that?" he asks, before the waiter swings by to ask, "Another round?"

"I'm good," I reply, to both men. Because I am. I'm so very good.

"Nah, we're all set for now," Daniel confirms.

"We should do this more often," I reply when it's just the two of us again.

"Go out?"

"Yeah. And also say nice things to each other. I like it."

"You're an easy person to say nice things about. Because I like *you*," he counters.

"You're going to give *me* a big head if you keep talking like that."

"Good. I like your head."

The double entendre lands perfectly. An attempt to cough can't cover up my giggle, and soon he's chuckling too, and then we're ensnared by can't-breathe, can't-talk, tears-leaking, gasping laughter, which holds us hostage until it decides it's done with us.

And I think, *what a beautiful night.*

And it is.

Day 8

Kiss in your car (nothing further!)

"Front seat or back?" Daniel asks as we stand in the garage next to his gray Lexus. It felt like the sexier choice than my SUV, which is littered with Cheerio dust, though that would've given us more room. Although, maybe less room is a win, in this instance.

"Considering it says 'nothing further,' I think the front seat is fine," I reply. I walk around to the passenger side and open the door to slide in. In years' past, it would've bothered me that Daniel didn't come around to open the door for me. Today, I'm just happy to get out of the cold air of the garage.

Daniel hops in, opens the garage and turns on the engine. I bring my hands in front of the vents to warm them, and he places the baby monitor on the dash.

"It'll get warmer in a minute," he says.

In a minute, we're supposed to be kissing.

"So how do you want to do this?" I ask. We've obviously kissed in a car before—that can't-get-enough, please-just-one-more-kiss frantic style of making out you do in the dating stage before you get dropped at your door. We've never made out in *this* car, though. The previous experiences were in Daniel's 2005 Saturn, which smelled like stale french fries and had a cassette player adapter that we'd connect to a classic iPod via the headphone jack. It's been a minute.

"We know how to kiss, Molls," he replies, turning his trunk to face me. "This isn't hard." With that, he reaches over, pushes a piece of stray hair behind my ear, and cradles my jaw in his hand. I lean into his palm, the way his thumb brushes over my cheek. One, two, three times. It's a familiar comfort. It sets my spirit at ease.

Without much thought, I shift toward him and press my lips to his. They're soft, more pillowy than any man has a right to have. Women pay good money for the sort of volume he has naturally. Almost immediately, we slip into a routine we choreographed a decade ago. Muscle memory pulls his bottom lip between mine, and my tongue seeks his in quick succession. An occasional nibble, a lingering suck, Daniel's hand tangled in my hair behind my ear. I couldn't write the steps in order, but that's okay. We know the dance by heart.

The console between us is an awkward divider, but we kiss anyway, until we reach the point where we'd normally move on to bigger and better and harder and wetter things. But tonight, we're in the car, with a "nothing more" rule. Do we just keep kissing?

"You're still the best kisser I've ever had. You know that, right?" he asks, after pulling away.

"Considering you haven't kissed anyone new since you first told me, I'd hope so." The words tumble out on a laugh. "You are also an excellent kisser. I wouldn't have married you otherwise," I joke, and I'm tickled to see a hint of pink appear on Daniel's cheeks. It makes him look younger. Boyish.

"So, did we complete the task, or do you think we're supposed to kiss longer?" he asks.

"I think that's the wrong question."

"Do you?" He tilts his head, trying to project confusion he doesn't actually feel.

"Yeah, I think the real question is, do we *want* to kiss longer?"

"If the alternative is going back inside and rotting our brains about the state of the world, I think kissing is a better idea," he says.

I have to agree. Plus there's something intriguing about finding out what happens after the music stops, so to speak. Are there more moves yet to be learned?

"What if you come over here?" he says, and there's a vulnerability in the ask.

The wheels in my head turn. "You want me to sit in your lap?"

"Sit, straddle, whatever."

I briefly consider climbing over the center console before an image stops me, one with my legs swinging over and hitting Daniel in the head and having to scoot my butt across the cold leather. I decide to get out and come around instead. This time, he leans over and opens the door for me. Next, he finds the button on the side of the leather seat that moves the chair as far from the steering wheel as it will go and presses it until it stops.

"Want some music?" he asks.

"Sure," I reply. He cues up something a little jazzy, a little sexy.

I duck under the car's frame and bring one knee to the side of his thigh before pulling up the other. Hear me say this: straddling a man in the front seat of his car is more difficult at thirty-two than it is at twenty-five. I swear I heard my knees creak just now.

"I don't know about you, but I'm pretty comfortable," he says, and it's too easy to ruffle up his hair with my hand and roll my eyes. It's an inside joke, one he made when I complained about my wedding shoes rubbing a blister on my heels, and the Cervadil opening my cervix when I was in labor, and long before that, the way the springs in my parent's sofa bed dug into my back when trying to sleep. As an outsider, the comment seems flippant, taunting even. But inside the relationship—and this car—it's a nod to our shared history.

"Shut up," I reply.

"Why don't you shut me up?"

This playful needling as foreplay is Daniel Hayes's specialty. It's never failed to work on me.

"Don't threaten me with a good time," I reply.

"Is the good time in the car with us? Or...?"

"You're insufferable."

"You love me," he says.

"I do."

With that, he brings both hands to my face and pulls my mouth toward his. I try my hands on the armrests and then his shoulders before dropping them to his upper thighs, where they stay. The kiss starts slow, languid, with some teasing mixed in. We settle into a rhythm that's not quite the usual but flows with the jazz lilting in the background. I ignore the press of the steering wheel against my lower back until I can't anymore, and shift my weight to reposition.

Daniel sucks in a breath as he breaks from the kiss, then says, "Feel free to do that again."

I drag my hips in a purposeful grind against the soft flannel of his pj pants and I can feel him hardening beneath me in real time. I do it again just to watch him flutter his eyes closed. His hands grip the flesh at the top of my ass.

"You're trouble," he says.

"You asked for it," I reply.

He gives a muffled "mmm-hmm," before bringing his mouth back to mine. It's more frantic than before, faster and deeper. Am I breaking the *nothing further* rule by continuing to grind against his lap? I don't care because it feels good. Easy. Like fun. It feels like being twenty-four with no re-sponsibilities.

Until a cry echoes from the baby monitor. It's like a cold bucket of water tipped over our heads, drenching us in the reminder that fun and easy isn't where we live anymore.

I bring my forehead to his chest, resting against his worn shirt and feeling the thump of his heartbeat for just a moment.

He holds me there, his hand splayed against the back of my head while he takes a deep breath. Then he whispers, "Duty calls," and taps twice on my hip. Oh right—he can't get up until I do. I shimmy backwards and he reaches for the door, until I can drag one leg and place it awkwardly on the ground while I try to maneuver the rest of my body in a tight twist to escape under the frame.

He follows behind, and I don't miss the way he adjusts his pants when he stands.

"You want me to get her?" he asks.

"Nah, I want the snuggles," I reply with a shrug.

He grabs my hand as we walk toward the door, and there's delight in how the simple affections lifts my spirits. "I liked that," Daniel says before I break off for Violet's room. "Like I said—best kisser."

"Maybe we should try it again sometime," I whisper in the dark as I release his hand. "I liked it too."

Day 9

Discuss your favorite past date, and how you'd modify it (if at all).

I thought dinnertime would be easier as Violet got older but until she learns to keep a spoon upright while bringing it to her mouth, I think I'm out of luck. There's yogurt on her tray, her shirt, her hair, the floor, the table, and Daniel's arm which he has resting too close to the line of fire.

"You're going to smell like sour milk if you're not careful," I say. He turns to meet my gaze and his eyes are soft. His chocolate brown irises are more milk than dark in this light. "It's a risk I'm willing to take to keep this girl happy," he replies before scooting his chair even closer to her.

I didn't know what to expect from him when I got pregnant. I knew he'd be thrilled—he's talked about being a dad ever since our first date. But with the demands of his job, and being estranged from his own parents, I worried. I wondered how he'd manage our relationship and another one (with an exceedingly demanding little being, at that) with everything else on his plate. I questioned if he'd still feel like mine, or if I'd still feel like his, or if we'd both feel like hers.

It was fair to worry that things would change, because they have. I feel more like *mom* than *wife* most days. But watching Daniel being Dad? It's a thrill I don't know how to put words to. He is so patient, so engaged. He's so *good* with her. When she was born, a secret paternal light switch flicked on and it often brightens the path for me, as sometimes I think I lack the maternal equivalent.

"It's good, isn't it, Lettie?" he says with affection dripping from his tone.

That's his special nickname for her and I often wonder if it's what she'll go by when she's old enough to choose.

She replies with a squeal of delight that turns Daniel's light brighter.

"How did we get the best one?" he asks me.

"The best baby?"

"Yep," he turns back to her, "the very best baby in the entire world right here."

"Well, when two people love each other very much…" I joke, and he nudges me under the table with his foot.

Tonight feels easy, like we're living the good old days right now. When I'm eighty-four and Violet is fifty-two, and her baby has a baby, I think I'll look back and be wistful for this very moment.

"We could've made another one if we'd stayed in the car last night," he volleys back.

"Nope, sorry, against the rules."

"The card game? Or yours?"

"Both. Shop's closed for the foreseeable future. Needs maintenance," I reply with a laugh.

"I can help with that!" he offers.

"Why don't you get today's card and we can work on the *emotional* maintenance first."

He reaches beyond the baby wipes in the center of the table to pull the card from the deck.

"Alright Molls—what's your favorite date we've been on, and would you change anything about it?"

"Dang, no kissing today? It's always one step forward, two steps back with these," I say.

"Should we peek at tomorrow's?" he asks.

"Absolutely not. The mystery is part of the fun."

"Fine enough. Favorite date—go."

My mind whirls with a near decade of memories. Concerts, trips, fancy nights out and cozy nights in. It's wild how much life we've lived together when I scroll through it like this. I land on one particular date, early in our relationship, and it's so predictable I feel myself cringe.

"It's that night at the fair, isn't it?" he asks, and I nod.

"Mine too. I think about it a lot, actually—about what made that night so great. It had everything we loved as kids—fried dough, rides that weren't quite up to safety standards, fireworks, those lemonade shake-ups—plus the freedom of having adult money and no curfew. Add the blissful bubble of a new relationship and that night was like dopamine on steroids." His face brightens with the memory, his hard-earned smile lines deepening.

"Dopamine on steroids," I chuckle. "That's exactly right. It was total sensory overwhelm. The lights, the smells, all the people pressing in, the crackle of the fireworks. Remember we tried to time a kiss to each boom?"

"Of course, because that was my idea. I wanted an excuse to kiss you. By making it a game, I bought myself about thirty kisses."

"I would've kissed you anyway, you dork," I reply.

"But then we would've missed the fun of watching the fireworks and *creating our own*."

"Oh my god, you're ridiculous."

"And yet, you married me." He lifts his glass in a faux salute.

Violet coos and Daniel adds, to her directly, "And now we have you, don't we? Who knows, without the firework game maybe Mommy would've been bored of me."

I roll my eyes but ask, "So would you change anything, looking back?"

"No, I wouldn't. It was perfect, as far as I'm concerned."

"You wouldn't sit out The Gravitron and spare yourself the embarrassment of puking in the trash can after? That was like our fourth date. It was a bit early for that sort of thing."

"Nope. I'd do it all again *exactly* as we did it, because it led us right here."

He looks at me, he looks at Violet, and at my hand on the table before threading his fingers through mine. "Would you change anything?"

How do you compete with such a perfect answer?

"I guess not. Not if it would've changed the ending," I reply.

"We should bring Violet to the fair this summer. She'd like all the lights." To Violet, he says, "What do you think, Lettie? Want to pet the animals?"

She bangs both fists on the table and it's as close to a yes as he could ask for.

"Looks like it's settled," I say. "Hayes' family trip to the fair is booked. Maybe we should make it a tradition. We'll probably want to leave before the fireworks though."

"As long as I can still kiss you, I'm in."

Day 10

Have today's conversation naked—no touching each other!

Today would've been a good one to sit on the back patio I've been hesitant for us to build. It's surprisingly mild for early December, and the perfect night for a thick, fuzzy blanket, a mug of hot tea, and a space heater while the chill nips at your cheeks. Instead, we're back on the couch.

"Day ten, huh? We're getting good at this," Daniel says. We're more than a third of the way through the Amorous Advent challenge now. "Do you think it's working?"

"I guess I do. What about you?"

"I spent the entire workday thinking about you straddling me in the car and wishing we could go back to day eight, so yeah, I'd say it's working." He says this with a tilt of his head, a lock of salt and pepper hair falling over his forehead. His smile prompts the smallest flip of my stomach. It's not a kaleidoscope of butterflies, but the fluttering of a few is enough to make my cheeks grow warm.

"Yeah?"

"Absolutely. Do you realize how hot you are, Molls? I've been itching to get home since the minute I left this morning."

I want to believe him, but the truth is I haven't felt hot in almost two years. I turned thirty and got pregnant the same month, and since then, I've been a growing, crying, stretching, leaking, squishy mess. Nothing about my current body screams sexy. Especially when hidden under the threadbare t-shirt and drawstring shorts I was wearing the night before last.

"This?" he says, pulling on a piece of hair that's fallen out of my messy bun, "drives me crazy. And these?" he rubs his hands over my thighs, stopping to grip at the thickest part, "taunt me every single time you squat to pick up a toy or bend to load the dishwasher. This game where we do the activity on the card and then stop? It's killing me. I love it. I love *you* for suggesting this."

His praise washes over me like honey, his sweet words dripping down and clinging to my skin. I will them to stay when I grab the Day Ten card from the deck and turn it over.

"Have today's conversation naked (no touching each other!)" I read aloud. "Hmm. Okay."

"Hell yes," he says. He is bubbling with enthusiasm to see my naked body, the one I appraise in the mirror with nothing but criticism. Maybe his appreciation will rub off on me.

"If I'm not allowed to touch you, I can't sit here," Daniel says as he stands and walks to an adjacent armchair. He strips off his shirt and then his pants, first letting his belt fall to the floor and then stepping out of each leg. He meets my eyes before shucking off his boxers until he's fully bare. "Your turn," he prompts.

My hands turn heavy as I lift the hem of my shirt. This man has seen me naked hundreds of times. A thousand? But never like this, in the light, without the rush of adrenaline that typically makes this step a short layover to the main event. Sweeping the t-shirt over my head, I watch his eyes fall to my chest. He sucks in a pained breath that gives me the courage to continue. With one forceful push on the waistband of my pj pants, they pool on the floor along with my panties. My skin pebbles with goosebumps, from the cold or from Daniel's gaze. Both, most likely.

"Should we sit?" I ask. What's the protocol for a butt naked conversation on a leather couch? I grab my shirt and place it on top of the cushion and gesture for him to do the same. I'm not ruining the furniture for this.

He sits and I sit, and it isn't three seconds before he says, "Open your legs for me."

That phrase, a favorite his, had been in retirement. I guess, until tonight.

A rush of heat floods my cheeks, my chest, between my thighs. I let my knees fall open and watch as his eyes lock on my core. He's tense with restraint, and it chisels his features—the set of his jaw, a tightness in his chest and arms leading to clenched fists. Every muscle is taut. It's a miracle I don't see him twitch.

"You been working out?" I joke, and it's enough to turn down the heat on the simmering tension for a moment. I need to catch my breath.

"Like what you see?" he volleys back.

"I do. You've got great abs."

"You've got great tits."

My nipples tighten at the mention. "They're not what they used to be," I sigh with defeat.

"They're perfect. Can I tell you what I'd do with them if I was allowed to touch you?"

Oh.

This isn't—why did I think this card meant talking about our weekend plans or something, and being naked while doing it?

After waiting for a reply that doesn't come, he says, "I'd take a handful of each and start by rubbing my thumbs over your nipples. Slowly at first. You'd hate it." His laugh is light, playful, but the way his eyes darken is not. Desire curls low in my belly.

"You're a tease," I reply.

"You know I'm right. You wouldn't be able to stand it. After a few minutes you'd be begging for more."

"Says the guy with an erection just from talking about it." I gesture to his lap, where his cock stands at attention. "I won't accept any slander about *me* being the eager one."

"Oh yeah? How wet are you right now? Put your feet up so I can see."

The demand lands like sparks to every one of my nerve endings, hot and sharp. Alive.

This isn't a game we've played before. I think I *like* it.

With a devilish smile, I lift my feet and place them on the couch next to my butt. I bring my palms to my knees to pull them open farther.

"Fucking hell, Molls," he says as he leans back and brings a hand to his hair and pulls, like he's trying to release tension any way he can.

"Like what you see?" I parrot his earlier words.

"God, you're dripping. All that just for me?"

"Nah, today it's for me." I drop a hand between my legs and swipe a finger through my arousal before bringing it higher.

The groan he makes is downright choked. He's not used to this sort of confidence from me. I'm not either, but his reactions are turning me bold. I'm drunk on the power of watching him *suffer*.

"Are you allowed to do that? Touch yourself?"

"The card said…oh shit, that feels good," I moan, "no touching each other. I think self-play is allowed. Why, are you going to get yourself off by watching me?"

He grips himself and tugs once, then twice. Bringing a palm to his mouth, he spits in his hand before returning it to his cock. He shudders before meeting my eyes in challenge.

"I won't say no to watching you play with yourself. How about you put two fingers in for me and I'll pretend I'm the one stretching you out."

My heart is a pinball ricocheting through my chest. I bring my index finger to my opening and slide it in, keeping my thumb tight to my clit. Daniel's gaze meets mine and he nods. I slip my middle finger next to it. An *mmmmm* falls from my mouth and hums against my lips. Before I can close my eyes, I hear him grunt.

"No. Eyes on me, baby."

He's leaning back in the chair, tight quads holding still as he strokes. Up and down, squeezing himself into his fist with a heaving chest and blown pupils. I match his rhythm with my own thrusts. The wet smack of my fingers punctuates the silence.

"It doesn't come close to my cock, does it?" he asks, holding my gaze. "You wish I was filling you up, working you over."

"Mmm-hmm," I nod. "Keep...," I try to push out the words but they're thready. "Keep talking like that."

"Is it turning you on, baby? Hearing how good I would make you feel? How I'd give that hand a break by pinning it to the bed and then stuffing you full?"

The room starts spinning. I can't catch my breath. My fingers move faster, push deeper, and Daniel's words feel distant but I hear him say, "Come for me, baby. I want you throbbing and soaked, with my name in your mouth."

My orgasm is a detonation, rocketing through me and knocking me flat. For a few moments I'm missing from this world, wracked by pleasure so intense it's almost painful. When I come back to my body, I hear myself chant his name.

"Holy shit," he says between heaving breaths, and I clock the mess he's made on his stomach. I did that for him. The sight of this droopy, stretch-marked, dimpled body of mine experiencing pleasure made him come *hard*. The thought turns my heart buoyant, like a balloon in my chest.

It takes a minute for us to reorient. I hop off the couch and grab tissues from the kitchen; I clean myself up before handing him the box.

We don't talk as we get dressed, but before I turn to head to the bathroom, he envelops me in a hug. His heartbeat thumps against my cheek, and with every breath his stubble catches my hair. If a picture is worth a thousand words, this hug is worth three.

"I love you too," I say, before pulling away. "We *are* getting good at this."

Day 11

Talk about the first time you said "I love you."

Violet's barky cough started a few hours ago. The pediatrician on-call was disturbingly undisturbed, which floored me, because it sounds like she can barely breathe. The virus, Croup, that causes the distinctive barking sound is common during the winter months. He said it affects infants more obviously because of their narrower airways. The treatment, provided there aren't retractions when she inhales, is cold air—something about vasoconstriction and relaxing the muscles in the neck.

Always a rule follower, this is how I convinced Daniel to take a walk at 9 p.m. Now we're walking through the neighborhood in the dark, bundled from head to toe, with a baby who sounds like a seal.

"The doctor did suggest we could open the freezer door and hold her in front of it," he says as he navigates the stroller around a bush that extends into the sidewalk.

"And how long could we sustain that? This will be better."

"Is the plan to walk all night, or…?"

"Let's stay outside until her stridor goes away or her breathing seems less labored. I can stay up if I need to," I reply.

The reality of parenthood is that no two days are the same. You might find yourself engaging in mutual masturbation one night and then pacing in the dark with a sick kid the next. This switching between realities gives me whiplash sometimes. I never know which version of Molly will be called up.

"If we're doing this for a while, should we tackle the next card? I brought it with me," Daniel says.

It's a welcome surprise every time he takes ownership to keep this experiment going.

"But what if it's more naked stuff?" I ask. "I'm not willing to strip when it's thirty-eight degrees out here."

"The physical prompts seem to be every other day. I bet tonight's will be a discussion card."

He takes his phone and the card out of the pocket, turns on the flashlight, and reads.

"Oh, this is no problem. *Talk about the first time you said "I love you."* See, told you—no nudity. Maybe tomorrow; let's hope the trend continues." He bumps his shoulder into mine with a chuckle.

Violet interrupts the moment with another forceful cough. I wince and then check on her, this precious little girl who could not be less interested in sleeping even though it's two hours past bedtime. I'm praying the cold air and the movement will relax her enough to pass out.

"I know we said I love you the same day," Daniel offers, "but I'm not sure who went first. Maybe you?"

"Definitely me. I kept waiting for you to say it, and I had this stupid idea based on gender roles that I shouldn't say it before you. So I waited, and waited, and when you weren't saying it, I snapped. I couldn't keep it in any longer."

"Ah, you're right. It was my apartment on Jefferson with the green suede sofa. You had convinced me to watch How I Met Your Mother—thank you for that, by the way; excellent taste on your part—and pretty soon we were making out."

"That always seemed to be the natural conclusion when we were at that apartment," I reply with a laugh that tickles my nose. "The memory of that night is really clear for me. You were laying down and I was between your legs, and I pulled away from the kiss and blurted it. The moment after felt frozen while I waited for you to say something."

"Kind of like when you didn't say yes to my proposal for nine whole seconds while I was down on my knee?"

I roll my eyes, though it's too dark for him to see it. "Come on!" I say, "I was shocked and overwhelmed. My *yes* came out as quickly as it could."

"And I said I love you almost immediately after you did. In your relief, you collapsed on top of me which felt like a great outcome on my end." He brings a gloved hand to grasp mine, still pushing the stroller with the other.

"It's funny, because I remember feeling petulant that you said it so quickly. I thought it meant you were ready. And if you were ready, why didn't you say it first?"

"Wait, wait, wait," he says as he stops walking and turns to look at me. The moon casts his face in shadow. "You just said you had to wait for me to respond, and now you're saying I answered too quickly? You're a walking contradiction."

"I won't argue with that. Imagine living inside this brain. It's scary sometimes."

"It's a creative, complex, silly, and beautiful brain, and also my favorite. Don't be rude to it."

"No promises," I reply. I peek over the canopy to look at Violet and find she's finally, gloriously asleep.

"Mission accomplished," I say to Daniel.

He tips his face to see her and a smile creeps up his cheeks.

"What do you think those kids on the green couch would say about us now?" he asks. "I think they'd be horrified we moved to the suburbs." It's accompanied by a laugh that he quickly quiets.

"You would've spent the last eight years in mourning if you'd known the gray was coming for your hair this early," I answer.

He huffs in agreement. "Sometimes it's hard to believe those people were us, and that we grew into this version. I think they'd be proud that we figured it out."

"*Have* we figured it out?" I ask.

"I think we're closer than we've been, and that feels like more than enough."

As we round the corner to our street, I let his words linger. We *are* closer than we've been. As silly and frustrating as these daily cards are, we've had more honest communication and more freely-given affection in the past week and a half than in the past year.

"I think you're right."

Day 12

Explore what feels good to your partner using only your hands.

"Let's consider this a do-over of day six," I say as I sit on Daniel's butt. He's lying face down in bed, shirtless and groaning as I knead the muscles in his back. "That one didn't count cause we were fighting. Let's hope we can get through this one without Violet's cough starting up again."

"She'll be fine…and I'm not complaining," he replies, but it's muffled by the pillow under his cheek.

"Of course not, you're the one getting the massage."

"For now. I'll get my hands on you later."

The words prompt a swoop in my belly; they're both a threat and a promise. And after the night we had on day ten, I'm eager for either, both, anything. Ever since, pieces of memory hit like lightning strikes. I'll be picking up the dry cleaning and get a flash of Daniel spitting in his palm, or folding Violet's tiny laundry and hear his *eyes on me, baby*.

It's a problem.

It's *distracting*.

And this PG-rated massage isn't nearly enough.

"Ooomph, that knot's been there forever, you don't have to fix it tonight," he says, and I realize I've been digging my fingers too deep around his shoulder blade. I switch to scratching and run my fingernails along his back. It leaves red, raised track marks, parallel lines that brand him as mine. He used to wake up every Saturday with them—evidence of a *productive* night before.

"Okay, my turn," he says.

"You sure?"

"Fully. Come here."

He scrambles up the bed, leans his back against the headboard, and pats the spot between his open legs. I shuffle over and sit, my back to his front.

"Can I take this off?" he asks while tugging at my shirt, with no hint of presumption or pressure. It's sweet. But I'm not feeling sweet.

"Please."

He says, "Arms up," and gently lifts the shirt from my body before tossing it on the floor. The cool air on my naked skin makes me shiver. The warmth of his palms landing on my shoulders helps.

"That's better," he says, and starts working. Firm swipes of his thumb to the base of my neck, then gripping my shoulders to press his fingers there. I can feel some of my tension melt with the pressure.

"Much better," I reply.

"You know, if the card didn't say hands-only, I'd kiss your neck right now. That's one of my favorite things about having you in front of me like this—nuzzling right here." He runs the back of his hand down the length of my neck before stopping at my collarbone. "This spot in particular."

I lean my head on his hand for a moment. "I'd like that."

He continues kneading the muscles in my back, this time near my spine. I let out a soft whimper when he hits a tender spot.

"Too much?" he says.

"Just a little sore."

"I'm trying to make you feel *good* tonight. Let me try something different." With this, he straightens, puts his hands on my hips and pulls me flush against him.

It's not an ideal position for a back massage, but apparently Daniel's done with that anyway. Instead, he brings his hands to cup my breasts. "This alright?" he asks, and the proximity of his mouth to my ear has his breath tickling my skin. I suck in a breath and then nod. "Thank fuck because I've been dying for this since we talked about it the other night." Just as he promised then, he swipes his thumbs over my nipples. Slowly, methodically, until it feels like torture. My back arches into him as I chase more contact.

"Told you you'd be begging," he says, and while I can't see his face, his tone is smug. Absolutely dripping with it.

"Hmm, pretty sure I haven't said a thing."

"Not yet. But you will. I know your tells."

As if to punctuate the point, he twists both nipples—hard. My gasp comes out half-moan. I love when he does that. He knows it, and does it again.

It's not long before he has me squirming. He palms my breasts, pinches and pulls my nipples, twiddles them between his index and pointer fingers. He runs a flat palm back and forth over my chest until the friction starts to sting. He pushes my tits together and describes, in *explicit* detail, what he would do with his mouth and where he'd put his cock if he could. And all the while, I am getting increasingly keyed up until the ache between my legs turns into a painful thrumming.

"Okay, I'll beg," I plead.

"What was that, baby?" Daniel taunts.

"Please, I need more. Lower."

"You want me to touch you here?" He brings a hand to cup my center, before drawing one finger from my entrance straight up my slit. It makes my breath stutter. "Yeah, that's what you want. You're needy for it, aren't you? I'll give it to you, baby."

Holding me tight against him with one hand still on my breast, he presses his thumb to my clit. The sensation is loud and then lingering, like a firework from our perfect date, one that pops and then fizzes its way down.

He finds a rhythm then, coating his fingers in my arousal, pushing inside me to curl against my inner walls, and then dragging them up to my clit, where he circles. He works my nipple in tandem, pinching, squeezing, twisting. It's *so much.* *It's so good.*

I'm floating, letting myself sink into the rhythm and be rocked by it. Slow and steady, I climb. He plays my body like a score played by ear. He's fluent in the language of my sighs.

Which is why his slap to my pussy—hard enough to sting, gentle enough to be loving—has me gasping. In surprise, but also from pleasure. "Again," I ask as my head lolls back to rest on his chest.

He flicks his wrist for another sharp slap and my god, it's lovely and confusing and dirty and exactly what I need. My quiet "yes," is tempered by a moan as he presses the heel of his palm against my clit. I'm sensitive in a way I've never been after the more forceful contact. The pressure of his hand there, the rough way he toys with my nipple, the two fingers he dips inside me, it's perfect, perfect and then I tip over the edge with the filthiest encouragement from this man's mouth—I catch *slut* and *come* and *mine* before I'm lost to this bed and this room.

Bright and diffuse.

Warm.

I'm falling like stardust, pinpricks of light tumbling through the universe until Daniel grounds me. His hand cups me again, and I flutter against his fingers.

"Too much," I say while twisting away from his touch. The sensitivity is unreal. "And it's your turn anyway."

"Not until I'm done," he replies, while he slides the pad of his thumb across my clit, in a featherlight touch. "You can give me another."

I want to argue that I can't, that I'm spent, that maybe I'm dying and the last orgasm was my final, gasping breath but when he holds his thumb with delicious pressure, my lips won't open for words. Only a moan.

"That's right, baby. Give me another."

Day 13

What is your biggest pet peeve with your partner?

"Oh boy, this should be fun," Daniel says as he tosses the card to me. We're sitting in bed, having anticipated another intimate prompt since they're becoming more frequent. Instead, I'm greeted with the worst question possible.

"Don't you think this might make us less close? There's a high likelihood I'll wake up tomorrow still frustrated by what you say tonight." I've always been risk averse. Oldest daughter, people pleaser, and—as I've noted before—a rule follower. I don't like conflict. I especially don't like it with Daniel because he's entirely too logical. Sometimes I just need him to listen. Maybe that's my biggest pet peeve.

He interrupts my spiral to say, "Getting our grievances out in the open is always better than stewing on them. And these are pet peeves, not final straws. It doesn't have to be too deep."

"What even is a pet peeve? Obviously, I understand the question but who came up with the phrase? Pet sounds too friendly for peeve." After saying and hearing the word so many times in succession, it's starting to sound wrong.

"I wouldn't bet the house on it, but my guess is that pet means 'yours' or 'something you keep close' in this context, like it does for pet project. So, a pet peeve is the thing you are peeved about and can't get over."

Again, far too logical. And frankly, my question was rhetorical. Am I stalling? Yes. Do I care? Not particularly. I grab our hefty gray comforter and pull it further up my legs. We registered for it at Crate & Barrel, and my grandma got it for us as a wedding gift. Her card included a note about "the importance of time together in bed," which I have tried not to think about every day since.

"You seem peeved currently," Daniel says. "Do you want to start?"

I roll my eyes dramatically in response. "Sure. Let me think about the biggest."

The words come out sounding snarkier than intended—I just need a minute to sort through my strategy here. I could list the things that bother me in quick succession if asked: the way he pronounces 'miracle' as 'merical,' his choice to bring his smelly yardwork shoes into the house instead of leaving them in the garage, that he won't eat ground beef in any preparation (not because he's vegetarian, but because he's picky), the way his gray hair and smile lines make him look more handsome than ever while mine make me look haggard.

But the card today is asking for the biggest pet peeve. I take a deep breath and release it with a flood of words that come out with no strategy at all. "It feels like you can be flexible with your job when it benefits you, but when we need something from you, it's too busy at work."

Wow, yeah, that was big all right. The complaint that escaped has been bottled up in my chest for a year now.

"Straight for the jugular, then?" he says with a light laugh, but it's the kind meant to break tension, not to indicate humor. I could pull back, try to soften the way the sentiment landed, but instead, I double down.

"I don't understand how you are able to take a morning off to get your car serviced and detailed, or meet an old coworker for lunch, or get a haircut, but when I ask for something—like you coming home at 4 o'clock on Tuesday so I can go to a physical therapy appointment—you can never leave."

"I do so much for our family, Molls. I'm contributing the way I can, and when I get home, I'm all-hands-on-deck until Violet's asleep. The amount of housework and parenting I do is way more than anyone else in the office, and I know because we talk about it. If I have a meeting or a call, or if there's a deadline approaching, I can't just step away," he says. And then he hammers the nail into the tender flesh of my heart with, "Especially for something optional like physical therapy."

"Healthcare isn't optional, Dan! I gave my entire body for our baby, for the better part of a year, so we could have this family. So you could have a chance to be the kind of dad yours wasn't. I want to be able to run, jump and sneeze without peeing myself. Apparently, that's too much to ask."

"No, listen—that's not what I'm saying. It's not too much to ask to do PT, we just need to coordinate on the schedule. If you give me enough notice, I can probably work it in, barring anything unexpected coming up."

"I want to be able to rely on you," I reply. "Do you know what it's like being everyone else's safety net and having none of your own? If you need cookies for the company potluck, I make them. If the house needs attention, I schedule the technician. Violet needs new clothes? I know the right size. And yes, it seems silly, because these are easy enough tasks. That's not the problem. The problem is that I make sure everyone else's needs are met, and nobody looks out for mine."

"I make sure your needs are met!" he shouts in a whisper, to not wake the baby. "I pay our mortgage. I bring in the trash can every Thursday. I keep track of our investments and work with the accountant to submit our taxes on time. All of the yardwork? That's my job. More than that, I listen to you. It may not seem like it, but I really do. I'm trying my best. And my pet peeve is that you can't seem to recognize it."

Guilt is a familiar, heavy, sticky thing. It never strays far from its home in my chest and doesn't wait to make itself known when I've forgotten to feel it. Right now, my guilt is performing a baton routine—sharp stabs of it against my ribs.

"I'm sorry, I…I know you do a lot. I didn't mean for this to become a game of who-does-more. To be honest, I'm jealous that you get to have autonomy. You can get a haircut when you want and don't have to ask for permission for it. My time is never my own anymore." Tears start to fall against my will, wet tracks streaking my face. "We used to be on parallel paths and then we had a baby and your life looks 90% the same and mine is unrecognizable. When it seems like you have flexibility, and you're using that time for yourself when I don't have any time, it makes me angry."

Daniel scoots closer in bed and wraps his arms around my shoulders. Pulling me to his chest, he brings a hand to cradle the back of my head.

"If you need time for yourself, we can make that time, Molls. It might not be on a workday, but I can take Violet on Saturday mornings so you can have some flexibility. We can do that," he says.

The tears keep coming, and my guilt dances an encore at the way I'm snotting all over his shirt. "You sure?"

"Yes. I want our little family to get what they need. Not just me and Violet, but you too. I'm sorry I haven't offered before, that I didn't see your need for it. That's my fault," he says.

"I'm sorry for making you feel like what you're doing isn't enough. You're a great dad, Dan. Truly. And you're right, you listen. We are two lucky girls to have you."

"Even when I fuck up?" he asks.

"Especially then, because you always make it right. And you are patient when I screw up, which happens way too often."

"I think you're perfect."

"I think you're full of shit," I say on a snotty laugh. "Can we be done now? This card sucked."

"Did it? Because you just got yourself a massage on Saturday."

"What are you talking about? We've already done two massage cards," I say.

"I'm booking you a real one while I take Violet to do some Christmas shopping. Just decided, and I won't take no for an answer."

"Then I'll happily say yes."

Day 14

Explore what feels good to your partner using only your mouths.

(After, read the Day 15 card to make any necessary plans for tomorrow.)

I swear, the real goal of this Amorous Advent challenge is not to reconnect but rather to build so much sexual tension that you can't help but climb each other when the time comes. Now that the daily prompts have been getting more physical, we've stopped our usual twice-weekly sex schedule. It's been eight days without it and while sex is never something I've actively craved, the limits on what the deck allows have me as riled up as a teenage boy. I've spent the entire day buzzing with want, wondering if today is the day we'll get to indulge. Somehow, I forgot what it's like to be sexually frustrated, to choose to stop before the end.

There's something maddeningly hot about it.

"Only mouths, huh? I can work with that," Daniel says as he places the card on his nightstand. "Does that mean I have to take off your clothes with my teeth?" His smile is a comfort—a soft place to land. His eyes, though, are devilish as they reflect glimpses of light from the windows. He's not kidding around.

"I don't have the patience," I reply as I strip my tank over my head and push down my shorts until I can kick them off the bed. I'm fully nude in fifteen seconds, and I find myself reaching for him, only to remember hands are off-limits.

"Looks like someone's eager."

"Don't act like you're not," I say as I nod to the sheet he's crawled under, tented above his lap.

"Less talking with that mouth."

He says it as brings himself to lay between my knees, resting his hands on either side of my hips as he draws one of my nipples into his mouth. It elicits a gasp, to which he replies, "Much better, baby." I slide down until I'm laying under him. The weight of his erection lands on my thigh.

This man's tongue is magic. He swirls languidly, then sucks hard before catching the peak between his teeth. He looks up from under his lashes to find my gaze as he slowly tugs. I watch my flesh stretch and feel a glorious pinch of pain as his teeth mark my skin. When he doesn't relent, but instead holds me taut and flicks his tongue over the sensitive tip, I moan. Not a whimper or a breathy plea, but a guttural moan. Primal. He answers by releasing me from his mouth, only to swipe a flat tongue, hot and wet, right where he left. He blows a breath on the tender skin which prompts a full body shiver. I'm so fucking lit up. The thought that I might come if he keeps this up, without ever touching my clit, is a revelation.

I strain against the desire to beg for more. I want my hands in his hair. I want his hand on my throat. I need his fingers between my legs.

If every option was on the table, my mind would bounce from one sensation to another—his mouth on my chest, my body stretching as he fills me, my hands scraping down his back. Tonight, my entire world exists at the intersection of his lips and my tit. I can do nothing but sink into the pleasure and try to tolerate the incessant, visceral need thrumming in my blood. Like holding my breath, the need balloons. It clamors at my chest, threatening for release. When Daniel groans and then sucks so hard my nipple will bruise, it escapes.

It crashes into me like a tidal wave, smacking the air from my lungs and then pulling me under. I have a vague sense of my body trembling as I lull back and forth under the waves. They're a comfort now. I exist entirely outside of myself and Daniel and his mouth. I'm weightless.

"Holy shit," I hear him say. Holy indeed—I think I ascended at one point.

The rustling of the sheets brings me back to life, to see Daniel shimmying down the bed and pressing soft kisses to my belly.

"Please, I need a taste, baby. Can I clean you up?"

I nod and pull up my legs so he can bury his face between them. He starts with slow, even strokes of his tongue, then with gentle sucks to my clit. The way he sighs, content like I'm giving *him* a gift, settles into my bones. They're filled with years of those sighs; they sit heavy with his praise. He deserves the same.

"Trade me," I say, breaking free from his mouth and crawling to where he sits. I angle my head to where I'd been laying.

"I wasn't done!" he protests, but he scoots himself to lay on his back nonetheless.

"Do you…want to keep going while I suck you?" I ask. It's been years since we've done sixty-nine, and never once, in eight years of marriage, have I proposed it. But if we're limited to our mouths, and I can't get my fill of him the way I want, maybe it'll be fun.

His "fuck yes," emboldens me to bring my legs on either side of his chest.

"Back up and sit, Molls," he demands, and I don't have time to be self-conscious about my postpartum belly skin that hangs between our bodies because he dives into my pussy like he can't wait another second. With my hands braced on the mattress, I let my moan vibrate around his cock as I take it into my mouth. With him warm and heavy against my tongue, I bob slowly, dragging along the vein that runs the underside. At the tip, I grip my lips and suck hard, then slide all the way down so he's hitting the back of my throat. When I gag, he dives into my entrance to feed more of himself to my body, to fill me with him from end to end and everywhere between. My arms buckle and he pushes deeper—his tongue in my cunt and his cock down my throat.

I rock myself back, brushing against the stubble of his chin while dragging my teeth along his shaft. "Keep it up, baby" I hear him say, and my hips start to drag my wet pussy against his face in rhythm. I match the speed with my sucks, taking him deep and pulling up, my tongue licking around the tip before diving back down.

"Yes, yes, baby, shit, yes, shit!" he says and I'm echoing the words as we both build toward climax. With a series of quick flicks against my clit, I fall over first, and a second later his warm, salty release coats my tongue. Without thought, I collapse on top of him and let the endorphins settle. I hold his cum in my mouth until I can force my jelly legs to move, until I can turn around and see his face when I swallow. I lick the remainder off my lips while his eyes trace the movement of my tongue with reverence.

"That was incredible, holy shit," he says, and I clock the sweat marking his brow and glistening in tiny pinpricks on his chest. The shiny coat of my arousal lingering above his lips.

"That was something," I reply, while a pointy edge of desire pokes around low in my stomach. While it's been softened by the orgasms, it's still sharp. It needs to be filed—or is it defiled? "I wish we could do more."

"You drained all the life out of me with that," he laughs. "But I can work you over again if you need it."

"Should we see what we're doing tomorrow, first? If the prompt is a good one, I can wait."

I reach to my nightstand and steal the next card from the deck. With a smile, I read it to Daniel.

"Yeah, babe. I can wait," I answer.

Day 15

Celebrate with a night out together. You select what the other wears.

It turns out I can't wait. Last night was…I don't even know how to describe it. I couldn't call my mom fast enough this morning to ask her to babysit today. I have never felt this much impatience and anticipation, not even for our wedding night (which turned out to be lackluster anyway on account of being tired, hungry, and beyond buzzed). I'm on edge, tense, flustered—my mom asked what had me so *atwitter*

when I begged her to stay with Violet tonight. Overnight. Like a jack-in-the-box with the crank turned and turned and turned, I'm wound up.

When Daniel comes behind me to plant a kiss on my neck as I plate Violet's dinner, I almost jump out of my skin. Not because I'm repulsed, but because my nerves are on a hair trigger. He smooths his hands down my arms with firm pressure, which helps, until he reaches into my waistband and uses his pointer finger to snap the band of the red, crotchless panties he set out for me to wear. My heart rate ratchets up even further.

"She said she'd be here at 5:30pm?" he asks. I shiver at the warmth of his breath against my skin.

"Yeah, any minute now. Can you…can you get Violet's overnight diaper and pjs and set them on the changing table?" The words come out breathless, which I need to fix before my mom arrives.

This low cut, black top from five years ago—which looked divine on my pre-baby boobs—isn't something I would've picked for myself at this age and stage. My mom will clock it immediately. Let's hope she doesn't notice the sheer lace bra that's not remotely restraining my nipples. And the cut-out underwear that has my arousal sticking to my inner thighs after one brush of Daniel's lips below my ear? It has me feeling like I'm a teenager again, trying to sneak out of the house with a flask of vodka tucked into a pair of early 2000s riding boots. I haven't tried to get something past my mom in decades.

The doorbell rings with its familiar chime, and Daniel rushes to answer. Thank God, because it gives me a minute to clear my throat and hype myself up with an internal pep talk about being a full-grown woman who can do what she wants.

"Hey, come in! We're thankful you could babysit again. I know Violet will be so glad to see you," he says.

"It's easy to say yes when you have such a sweet baby. Where is that little flower of mine?" she answers as Daniel takes her coat and hangs it in the hall closet.

"Molly was fixing her dinner—she's probably in her high chair. You know how she gets when she's hungry."

"Who, Violet or Molly?" she asks, and it's the levity I need to welcome her without flushing red from cheeks to chest.

"Hey, we *both* come by it honestly!" I say, before reaching for a loose hug—one that won't have me pressing my nearly-bare chest into hers.

"Fed baby, loved baby is what I always say. Anything I need to know before I usher you two out the door?"

"I don't think so," Daniel replies. "Same bedtime routine as last week. You can give her a bath if this spaghetti dinner turns into a massacre."

"It very well might," I cut in.

"That's well and good with me. Now, you two go have fun. I'll see you in the morning!"

She raises a hand to shoo us toward the door as she sits at the table with a bubbly, babbling Violet. Our sweet girl who couldn't seem to care less that we're leaving.

"Thanks, Mom! Text if you need anything—seriously," I add.

She rolls her eyes and continues to shoo. With Daniel's hand on my lower back, we step into the garage to head out for our first night away since we became parents.

★★★

"I take it back—room service was the right choice," he says while holding a fry that's been dipped in aioli at one end.

"You're just saying that because I wouldn't be topless down at the bar."

"Yep, that's exactly right. This is better."

We're sitting in a king size bed at The Continental, arguably the nicest hotel in town, while stuffing our faces with $22 burgers and playing a no-cards game of strip poker. That is, we're removing layers when the other person asks. So far, Daniel has removed his sweater—my favorite of his that reminds me of the trip we took to Quebec City four years ago during the holidays—and pants. I've removed my blouse and skirt. My nipples strain against the thin mesh of the bra, though it can hardly be called such when it's more straps than fabric.

"What do you think? Better?" he asks.

"Any time I can eat a thousand calories of meat, cheese, and fried potatoes while staring at your abs is a win in my book. My dream is to not leave this bed for the next fourteen hours. That would be best of all."

"And what's the sleeping/not sleeping ratio in this dream of yours?" He takes a bite of his burger and sauce sticks to the corner of his lips. When I reach over to wipe it, he takes my finger into his mouth and gently sucks. It's the eye contact that kills me—those dark brown eyes, eager and earnest. He releases my finger with a wet pop.

"Hmmm, let's say ten hours for sleeping, four hours for other stuff."

"We can wrap up this dinner in the next ten minutes, then. Give ourselves more time for the *other stuff*," he replies. A smile twists at his lips, and it's almost shy. It would be if I didn't know better. "Start by losing the bra."

I hold his gaze as I reach behind me and unclasp the band. The slippery fabric falls to my waist and his eyes fall to my tits, which bounce from being released. The weight of his stare and the cool air from the wall unit have my nipples puckering instantly. The warmth of his mouth would soften them, and that sounds heavenly right now.

"Any chance you're already done?" I ask, as I lift my tray to the nightstand and push his away from his lap. "And take off your boxers."

He stands, grabs the tray and places it on the floor. His boxers follow suit as he says, "With dinner, yes. With you, not until you're begging me to stop."

"Is that a threat?" I tease, as he climbs back onto the bed.

"No, baby, that's a promise."

With one smooth motion, he grabs my waist and lifts me to straddle him. "These last few days, Molls, I thought I might die, not having you the way I wanted. It's been so good, and just enough. But I'm tired of just enough." He bends down to pull a nipple into his mouth and sucks hard. A throaty moan pours out of me. "I think you're tired of it too."

With his hands on my hips, he pushes me slowly down his length, then pulls me back, groaning, as he coats himself in the wetness that's been growing between my legs all night.

"Never get rid of these," he says as he snaps the band of the crotchless panties again. "The entire ride over here I was thinking about slipping my hand under your skirt and feeling for myself how eager you were. Knowing you were right there, this pussy exposed and dripping for me, it's a miracle I didn't crash the car."

"I would've let you, you know. Finger me on the ride. I would've loved it."

This time, his groan comes out tortured. I slide back and forth on his cock of my own volition and watch his Adam's apple bob as he swallows.

He grabs the hair at the back of my head in a fist, tugging until my eyes meet his. "You know what I've learned these past few days? You like being slutty for me. All those nights we spent going through the motions and *this* is what you needed. Isn't that right?"

My nod is accompanied by a whimper as he tilts my hips and grinds me against him, hard.

"Like I said the other day—I meet your needs. And you are needy tonight, baby. So needy."

If the prompts on the cards have unlocked a boldness in how I express myself with my body, they've done the same with Daniel's words. And God, it's working for us. The more aggressive I am, the dirtier he gets. The filthier his words, the more pliable I become. What if we'd spent our whole life, our whole marriage, never knowing this? Never exploring how free we can feel, not outside of our commitment but in it? Because of it?

Another slow, tortuous roll of my hips brings me back to the gaping want between my legs. "Please, fill me up. It's been too long," I ask.

"You know I will, but not yet, baby. I need to taste you first."

Before I can reply, he sits up, loops his arms under my thighs to lift them, and slides down the bed. He stops when my knees are on either side of his ears, my center hovering over face.

"God, this view. Do you know how pretty you are, all swollen and pink and wet like this? I can hardly stand it, knowing you're this worked up and I haven't even touched you yet. You're perfect," he says, and then lifts his head to lick one slow swipe up my core. "You taste perfect too. Now sit."

I'm about twenty pounds heavier than I was the last time we did this. He senses my hesitation and says, "Molly, if you don't sit I'm going to make you sit."

"But I don't want to crush you," I reply, self-conscious of my new body and what it might mean for this particular activity.

"*Please* crush me. Please crush that pretty little pussy into my face until the only thing I can breathe is your scent. Let me have it, Molls. Sit."

I won't argue with a man who is begging to pleasure me, so against my better judgement, I sit. I'm rewarded immediately with a groan that vibrates at my entrance. He spends the next few minutes exploring with his mouth and tongue, building up my need and never lingering long enough to meet it. He laps from my entrance to my clit, he sucks right there and flicks with his tongue, he dives into me and pulls back out just as quickly. Occasionally, he turns his head to bite at the flesh of my inner thighs. It's infuriating and wonderful and also, I might die if he keeps it up.

"Babe, please," I whine.

"Please what?" he answers from beneath me, when I recline just enough to spare his mouth.

"Please, make me come."

"That's what I wanted to hear. Of course, baby," he replies, before gripping my legs and diving back in with a fervor that steals my breath. What was once languid, leisurely, is now intentionally aggressive. He spreads me with his thumbs, leaving my sensitive clit entirely exposed to the thrashing of his tongue. He flicks in rhythm until I'm thrusting against his mouth, chanting *more* when I can catch a breath.

I stay just like that, riding his face, while he gives me the *more* I asked for. My orgasm hits like a slingshot, a quick, powerful release that has me careening over the side of a cliff at Mach 1. Holding onto his hair—probably too tightly—is the only thing keeping me grounded. I'm heaving breaths when I come back to myself, to sit on my heels with my heart slamming in my chest.

"Need a break?" Daniel asks.

I shake my head no, as words are still beyond my grasp.

"Good. You stay here." He slides himself down and out from under me and I collapse on the white fluff of the comforter, face down.

"Ass up, baby," he commands, and I feel his fingertips grip the hinge point of my butt and hips, tugging. I push up to my knees but leave my chest resting on the mattress.

"Can I take you like this?" The ask is a courtesy; he knows this is my favorite position.

"Always," I reply, and I mean it. If sex can be like this, the answer is always. Anytime. *Every* time. He brings his cock to slide against my throbbing center, wetting himself before he pushes in.

Achingly slow, he feeds his cock to my body, one inch at a time.

"I missed you," he says, as he lowers to press kisses on my spine while he fills me. "You feel like home. This," he punctuates with a thrust—finally—"feels like home."

And it does. His slow pull out of my body and immediate push back in feels as familiar as that favorite sweater. Comforting, warm, well-loved. For all the new we've been doing lately, there's something remarkably blissful about defaulting to what we know we like. It's a gift from all our years together, the way my body speaks to his, and his to mine, until the only replies are muffled moans.

He continues his pace, slow and then fast, gentle and then forceful, until he says, "You want a hand, baby?"

"Always," I repeat again, and he brings his fingers to the apex of my legs, just above where we're joined, to rub circles against my clit. If I weren't already half-collapsed, this would've done it.

"Mmm, that's it, that feels good doesn't it?" he asks, then answers himself with, "I know it does. You feel so fucking good, Molls. So fucking perfect. I see you trembling, are you going to come for me, baby? While I'm stretching you out and playing with you, like this?"

If the first orgasm was a slingshot, this one is a boomerang. I release, and release, and release, offering each one to the universe while it answers with another. I'm vaguely aware that Daniel's thrusts have become erratic, that he's cursing under his breath as he pounds into me, into my pussy that's squeezing him with muscle contractions he can barely withdraw from. The movement falters and then stops with a groan the entire hall must hear.

He pulses inside me, laying his chest against my back for several moments, before he pulls out. When I start to feel the wet stickiness of his release drip from me as I move to sit up, he stills me and pushes it back inside with two of his fingers. It's almost enough—almost—to make me ready to go again.

"You better hope my IUD is working," I laugh when I peel myself off the bed to head to the bathroom.

"Nah, *you* better hope your IUD is working. My part of conception is done," he jokes back.

When I've cleaned up and he's back in his boxers (and I realize my regret at not bringing a pair of fully-crotched underwear), we settle into bed and turn on the tv like we would at home. But this time, instead of sitting at opposite sides of the couch and intermittently scrolling on separate devices, I lean into him. I scoot my body until it fits into his, with my head on his chest and his arm around my shoulder.

This, too, feels like home. And I didn't realize until this month, how homesick I was for it.

Day 16

What do you wish your partner knew about you, or your life together?

Sometimes I think about military wives whose husbands deploy for months on end. Next, I think about wives of consultants, whose spouses are gone Monday through Thursday every week on assignment. Then, finally, I think about myself, and the single night away Daniel's had on the calendar for months, and try to guard against self-pity. Violet and I can handle a work trip for just one night.

I'm curled up in bed, nursing a hot mug of tea and scrolling aimlessly through the worst of the Internet when he calls. When I swipe to accept, my screen fills with my favorite picture, of the two of us in Spain six months post engagement. We look so carefree.

"Hey baby, sorry it's late," he says, but it's only 9 p.m. here.

"I'm up," I reply, and fiddle with a loose string on the edge of our comforter, twisting it around my finger and then sliding it off with my thumb. "How was it today?"

"Good. One of the better offsites I've attended—lots of stuff in the works. How are you? How's Lettie?"

"Also good. She was cracking me up today. You know those oranges we got in the holiday basket from your office? She's taken a liking to one. She may or may not be sleeping with it currently." My chuckle lilts, the tail of a kite caught in a breeze.

"She's going to wake up covered in pulp and juice," he replies.

"If she does, I'll give her a bath. She'll be the best-smelling baby at play group."

"And how about you? Miss me yet?"

"Terribly. The cards did us dirty giving us the best night yet, right before you skip town," I say.

"Super rude. They should've consulted with us," he laughs.

"Want to do today's? It's probably a talking prompt."

"No phone sex? What a missed opportunity."

"You're ridiculous," I say, while reaching to my nightstand and peeling the Day 16 card from the pile. "Alright, it says *what do you wish your partner knew about you, or your life together?*"

"Damn, definitely no phone sex."

"Nope, just good old-fashioned vulnerability. Wanna go first?" I ask.

"Hmm. This is difficult because you already know everything about me."

"Do I?" I taunt.

"You can't see it but I'm rolling my eyes right now," he says. "Hard."

I bite the corner of my lip because this back-and-forth banter, teasing each other like this, is fun. This is teenager-style flirting leftover from kissing in the car the other day. I like it.

Daniel clears his throat and says, "Okay, how about this. I…hmm…I, I worry every day that Violet will grow up and resent me because I didn't do a good enough job. That I'm going to look back and realize I'm as terrible as my dad was."

"Dan, no," I say, but he cuts me off.

"Sorry, let me just…I don't know how to be a good father, Molls. I'm winging it. There's no model for me—the bar from my family is low enough to step over. I'm trying my best, I think, but I worry it's not enough."

What I expected from the prompt today? This was not it. I've begged Daniel for years to open up about his dad and his upbringing. Seems the physical distance, that we don't have to look at each other while sharing, has finally made him willing.

"Do you want the good news or bad news first?" I ask in reply, knowing a list of platitudes about his ability won't placate him.

"Bad news," he says, just like I knew he would.

"We're definitely going to screw Violet up. She'll be in therapy someday talking about the ways we messed her up and the things we didn't deal with in ourselves that we projected to her. It's inevitable she leaves us with some damage."

"Is this supposed to be motivational? Because if so, you're doing a shit job of it," he says with an incredulous huff.

"No, but it's the truth. For me, that gives some freedom. We don't have to do this parenting thing perfectly. Even if we somehow did, she still wouldn't walk away unscathed. That's the nature of a relationship. We're imperfect people and we hurt each other sometimes, mostly unintentionally."

"And what's the good news?"

"Bad parents don't worry that they're bad parents. They don't take time to reflect on how they could be better. They're too focused on themselves. Do you think your dad ever stopped for a minute to evaluate his parenting performance and feel guilty? Absolutely not. *That's* what makes you different from your dad, and an infinitely better one. That, and about a million other reasons. Your desire to get it right is part of how you love Violet. And you love her so, so well, Dan. I'm pretty sure she loves you more than me, as a result."

His sniffles crackle in the speaker against my ear. "You mean that?" he asks.

"Every word. You're the best dad I know—truly. And not just because my sample size is small," I laugh. "I couldn't ask for a better partner and father for our family. We got the best one."

"*I* got the best ones," he replies, and I can hear him shifting positions, maybe stretching or reaching for a tissue. "Now, if we're done with my trauma dump, let's hear yours."

"Okay, this is tricky," I say, biding myself some time. "I already told you I get jealous of you sometimes, because your life looks mostly the same. But if I'm honest, even deeper than that, sometimes I feel my loss so acutely—the other Mollys I could've been if I'd picked a different path. I don't regret this one! Hardly ever," I chuckle, "but I feel homesick, almost, for who I could've been in those other universes. I could've been really great, you know." He tries to interject but I stop him to say, "And don't you try to say that I *am* really great! I'm doing important work, I know. It's just a small life, I guess. And those other lives could've been bigger."

"Do you want a bigger life?" he asks, quietly. Contemplatively.

"Sometimes. And maybe I can still have it, when Violet's older and we're done having babies and the brain fog finally—hopefully—lifts. But right now, my life is tedious. It's laundry and meal prep, cleaning up and her sleep routine, over and over on repeat. I could've been traveling or researching the cure to cancer or making a film, you know? Instead, I'm trying to wipe crusty boogers off of my baby's face while she screams."

"You hate flying, you dropped out of pre-med after one chemistry course, and you know nothing about movies," he says with a laugh. "I don't think those are dreams you're actually missing out on."

"First of all—rude," I reply, echoing his laugh but with a bit of added petulance. "Second, it's not about the dreams themselves. It's the loss of possibility, I guess."

"Why don't you take some time and write a list of how you might make your life ten percent bigger, with a goal that feels achievable in the next year. I may not be able to give you a lab or fly us to Europe for a month, but I can give you support—the time, at least—for you to grow. Those other Mollys are still in there, just buried. I think we should find them."

Now I'm the one blinking away tears, a few of them collecting against my lash line and threatening to fall. How could this man possibly think he isn't enough for us?

"I'd like that," I reply.

"We'll do it, then. And Molls?" he asks.

"Yeah?"

"Thanks for telling me. We should do this more often."

"How about another card tomorrow?" I offer.

"I can't wait," he replies.

Day 17

Share an intimate desire or sexual fantasy that your partner doesn't know.

"Well, won't this be fun?" Daniel says as he hands me the day's card. I skim it and heat rises in my blood. The electric blanket I finally put on the bed this morning and have set to eight isn't helping.

"It says *share*, not indulge, babe. This is another *talking* card."

"What do you want to bet tomorrow's prompt is the do-ing?"

"Want to check?" I ask.

"Nah, I like the surprise." He's sitting against the head-board, two pillows behind his back, without a shirt. The muscles in his abs flex as he breathes out a soft exhale. I could run my fingers along them and watch goosebumps trail in their wake. Except I can't, because it's a *talking* day.

"Are you pouting?" he says, his voice capturing the smile on his face.

"Was I? Just distracted by your abs. And now rude it is that I'm not going to get my hands on them tonight."

"I already know how much you love my abs. You're sup-posed to tell me something I *don't* know." The smirk he gives is equal parts flirty and infuriating.

Deciding to level the playing field, I peel off my top. Without the threadbare t-shirt I've had for ten years, I'm fully topless. "Now who's pouting? Or is it *panting*? You look short of breath."

"Nope, I'm fine," he says as he sucks in a lungful of air before biting down on a fist. "Let's get started."

"You go first," I prompt.

"What if it freaks you out? If you go first, then I'll know how wild I can be."

"What if *I* freak you out?" I volley back. "I could be into some really kinky stuff."

He cocks his head and looks me over, dragging his eyes from my waist, lingering at my tits, and perusing slowly upward before he meets my eyes. I feel it like his fingertips walking up my skin, and a shiver courses through me. "You could be. I believe that now," he says in response.

"It's not *that* kinky. It's probably pretty tame by everyone else's standards."

"So you have an idea in mind, then?"

Damn. I walked right into his trap to make me share first. I won't give him the satisfaction of the win, though, so I roll my shoulders back, jut out the girls, and look him right in the eye to say, "Tie me up."

Daniel chokes on his own saliva and tries to cover it with a cough. A creeping red flush starts on his neck.

"I want you to tie me up and blindfold me," I continue. "Then, I want you to do whatever you want. Take your time, play with me, surprise me. Use one of my toys or whatever you like. I'd want it to be time-bound though, so I'm not worried about whether you'll leave me there."

"Do you really think I'd get you restrained and consenting to whatever I want and then *leave*? Absolutely fucking not." I watch him reach below the comforter to adjust himself, though it doesn't stop the sheet from tenting above his lap. "Handcuffs, rope, or fabric ties?" he asks.

My skin prickles and the thumping of my heart travels between my legs, settling into a dull ache.

"Ties, I think."

"Mmm-hmm. Hands, feet or both?"

"Maybe hands to start," I reply. "I liked it when we couldn't use our hands a few days ago."

He nods and rolls out his shoulders. "Do you like the idea of not being able to touch me, or not being able to stop me? Obviously, we'd have a safe word you could use if it gets to be too much."

"I like the idea of being totally at your mercy. By the end of the day, I am tired of making ten thousand micro decisions—I want you to be in charge. I want you to make me feel good."

The ache grows in my core, wetness collecting in anticipation of a release that's not coming—not today at least.

"Do you want me to tell you what I'd do? Or is the anticipation part of the fun?" he asks.

"With the blindfold, I think the anticipation is part of it. So, what do you think? Was that too wild?" I reply.

"Not a chance. How about I raise the stakes and share my idea?"

"Should I be nervous?" I ask. He laughs and brings a warm hand to brush a piece of hair behind my ear. The contact, gentle and mild as it is, is electrically-charged. I want to tilt my head against his hand to trap it on my shoulder and keep him there. Instead, he pulls back.

"Nah, I don't think so," he says. "Remember on our honeymoon when I bent you over the balcony railing in our room? Maybe it's a voyeurism kink, but I like the idea of being public and the risk that someone sees exactly how feral you are."

I like the idea too. Except that I'm a mother, and getting arrested for public indecency is not a risk I'm willing to take. I tell Daniel as much, and he scrapes a hand across his jaw.

"What if we do both?" he continues. "I'll tie you up in the living room, fully exposed to the windows facing the rear of the house. If we do it tomorrow night, it'll be dark, but there's still a chance someone will be on the walking trail behind the yard. If they see us, they see us. We won't stop them from watching. *You* won't know if someone's watching."

Oh.

The windows Daniel's talking about aren't just windows—they're damn near a glass wall that spans the length of the room, overlooking the yard (and what could be, at some point, a back patio). The natural light from those massive windows is what sold me on this house.

"So what do you think, Molls? You in?" he asks, with a nudge of his shoulder against mine. I watch his eyes drop down to my breasts, and the hardened peaks of my nipples.

"I'm in. You figure out what we need."

Day 18

Try something adventurous you've never done.

There's a good chance this prompt was intended to mean *rock climbing* or maybe *a sushi making class* and not being tied up in front of a window. But after last night's conversation, the only thing on my mind is bringing Daniel's vision to life. I spent the day trying to force my brain from dwelling there because I was close to needing a different pair of panties before eleven a.m. Meanwhile, it was a normal day for Violet, who had no idea that after being safely put to bed, we'd turn the white noise machine to high so her dad could make a mess of me. The static hum emanating from her room dims as Daniel closes her door.

If there's a protocol for waiting to be tied up in your living room, I certainly don't know it. I changed into a robe and have nothing underneath, figuring I could at least take care of that part. After all, he's supposed to take care of the rest. That's part of the fantasy.

"Ready, baby?" he asks as he saunters into the space. He doesn't seem to share my nerves about doing this right. With one hand, he places a pile of ties—literal dress ties—on the couch while the other pops open the buttons on his shirt using his finger and thumb. "I've been thinking about this all day."

"Difficult, wasn't it?" I reply. "For me too."

"I love that you can't control yourself when I'm not here. What were you thinking about, exactly?" He shucks off his shirt and flicks open his belt, sliding it from his waist and dropping it on the floor. Maybe another day we could use that. As a restraint or…otherwise. *Who am I?* I don't know, but I like her. She can stay.

I untie the robe and let it fall open, baring my cleavage and giving him a straight line of sight to my pussy. My personal landscaping has taken a backseat to everyone else's needs this year, but today, I worked some magic thanks to a trimmer that was recommended by an exotic dancer on TikTok. I'm as bare as I've ever been. He exhales with a groan.

"Hmm, what was I thinking about today? Mostly this," I muse, while I drag a hand down my front. He grips my hand before I can touch myself.

"*This* is why I need to restrain you. This pussy is mine tonight." He walks me around to the side of the coffee table that faces the back wall, where he gestures to the floor. "Lay down, baby."

I hadn't considered exactly *how* I'd get tied up in the living room. Now it's obvious. Nodding, I sit before shimmying down to my back, until my hands are above my head in front of the table's legs. It was a good idea to keep the robe on; the floor is cold even through the terrycloth.

Without a word, Daniel grabs the ties and kneels in front of me. He takes care to massage my hand before wrapping the silky fabric around it and down my wrist, and then securing it to the heavy wood behind me. He does the same on the other side, then sits back on his heels, opens my robe until I'm entirely splayed before him, and groans. I'm keenly aware that the light is still on, which means I'm splayed for anyone who's out for an evening stroll. Equal parts bashful and energized by the thought, I squeeze my legs together.

"God, you're so pretty," he says before opening my legs, bringing two fingers to my entrance to wet them and dragging them up to my clit. As much as I wanted to be blindfolded, my hairs stand on end being able to look down and watch him play like this. His dark eyes are hooded, his lips drawn thin in concentration as he watches those fingers plunge inside me. The sudden pressure makes my back arch, and with the extension, my wrists tug at the ties.

Oh.

Yes.

Yes.

"Mmm hmm, you like it, baby?" Daniel says as he brings that same hand to sweep my hair away. With the other, he gently lifts my head and places a tie underneath. Wrapping it across my eyes, he doubles it over and then rests my head back to hold it in place. "This'll have to do for tonight. You're going to have to stay still."

"Yes, sir," I reply, and I mean that I'll be sure to behave, but with the ties and the blindfold and Daniel controlling my body, it comes out submissive. Based on his grunt and the way I can feel his cock bob against my thigh, he likes it.

With my eyes covered and my hands tied, I'm down two senses with three remarkably heightened. A breeze whispers against my skin every time he moves. The pull of his hand against his shaft—skin on skin, once, twice—is audible. I hear the shuffling of him between my legs, feel the warmth of his breath against my core and then the hot, hot slide of his tongue between my lips.

"Shit!" I exclaim.

"Baby, we're just getting started," he replies, and his laugh tickles my bare flesh. Then it's slow, lingering licks up my center, hard sucks at the apex, the occasional bite to the softness of my inner thighs. He stretches up to grip my breasts, and I imagine him in child's pose, relaxing himself by filling my negative space.

This is something I didn't expect tonight—without a destination for my hands or eyes, I'm trapped in my brain. There are only two choices: attend to my racing thoughts, or bring all of my focus to the sensations this man is creating for me. The second option is the only way forward.

Daniel continues carrying me up a slow ascent, meticulous in his attention to the parts of me that are throbbing for him. He tweaks my nipples, then slips a hand down my body to join his mouth, letting his fingers work my entrance while his tongue flicks at my clit. I can see us in my mind's eye, me naked and restrained, tugging at my ties, Daniel pumping into me and sucking at my clit until I'm trembling. It's not long before my chest is heaving and I'm just inches from the summit and I can almost taste the relief on my tongue…when he stops.

"What the fuck are you doing?" I plead, and I know it's not fair because I said he could do what he wants tonight but I didn't mean *this*. This is torture.

"I think you mean, what am I *not* doing," he replies with slippery sincerity that makes me want to strangle him. But of course, I can't.

Instead, I hear his knees crack—or maybe it's his ankles?—as he changes position. Then, in one smooth motion, he wraps his hands around my calves and lifts them to his shoulders. My hips tilt in response, lifting slightly off the floor. He runs his cock between my lips to wet it, and I whimper when the head makes contact with my swollen clit.

"All day, I thought about what I'd do tonight. I always knew I'd taste you—that was a given. But after that? Would I have you return the favor? Hover over you to suck me off?" He pushes forward, bending me in half with my legs nearly over my head until his cock touches my lips. I lick our combined arousal from his tip. He releases a guttural groan that vibrates against my thighs.

"But then I realized," he says, as he leans back and gives relief to the burning stretch in my hamstrings, "that what I wanted most of all was to fill you up, knowing that anyone who walks by will know that you're *mine*."

He brings his hands to the soft flesh of my hips and presses his fingertips there, stilling me. God, I need him inside of me. I need him to move. I need, I need, I need.

"Whose is this pussy, baby?" he asks, dragging his cock up and down the length of my pussy, getting so close to where I want him before retreating.

"Yours, it's yours," I stammer. I swear I can feel him nod.

Finally, he nudges his tip into my entrance and for a moment I'm washed in relief until the pulsing want threatens to swallow me whole as he lingers there, just an inch inside.

"Please, Daniel, please."

"Please what?"

"Fuck me. Stretch me, fill me, use me, just don't fucking stop," I reply. The words sound foreign to my ears; they come out in my voice but with someone else's bravado.

He leans down, again taking my legs with him and pushing them to my chest, to whisper, "That's my girl," before pushing inside. The slow, taunting, give-and-take of before is gone.

Now he's just giving.

After seating himself in my body, he uses my hips to slide me up and down his shaft. The drag of him against my inner walls, the sliding of my bare back against my nubby robe, the wet squelch of our bodies when he drives into me, the smell of sweat and sex makes me weak. It's all-consuming, like the world is spinning and the only anchor point is where we're joined.

"You feel so good, baby. So tight. I love watching you take me like this," he says, pulling out. "I love watching you stretch around my cock," he says, pushing in. "Watching me disappear into you. It's so,"

thrust,

"fucking,"

thrust,

"good."

thrust.

Each move of his hips is a punctuation mark—an exclamation point—for emphasis. I want to reply, to say *yes, so good*, but my mouth opens for a moan and nothing else. The whole world is blurry, even in my mind, within the darkness of my blindfold.

I hear it before I feel it, the click and then the buzzing of my favorite toy. On instinct, I try to reach for it, only to remember my hands are tied—literally. Daniel laughs.

"Don't worry, sweetheart, I know what to do with it," he says, and then the small bullet vibrator nudges my clit and a searing pulse of pleasure radiates through my body.

"Oh God, yes," I manage to reply between breaths.

He continues to fuck me, and it's all so much—the rhythm of him entering and retreating and the unrelenting hum against my clit, the few seconds every thrust where the stars align and he's pushing against me from the inside and out.

"More, please, more," I beg.

He turns the vibrator up—*holy shit*—and picks up his pace, rutting into me harder.

"Do you know how hot you are like this?" he says, and I don't feel sexy, I feel like a scattered collection of nerve endings, but still he continues, "Those pretty tits bounce every time I bury myself in your pussy. And down here," he tilts the toy slightly, eliciting a gasp, "you're swollen and dripping with want, Molls. You're stunning, baby. God, I'm so lucky."

And you'd think the dirty talk or the magnitude of different sensations would have pushed me over the edge but they don't. This time, it's his gratitude. His appreciation. *He feels so lucky.*

My release spills like liquid sunshine, warm and bright, curling my toes. In my haze, I ask Daniel to come, to be with me here, and he does.

After, he pulls out, lowers my legs and collapses next to me. Our breaths mingle while our bodies recover. His heart beats fast against my chest as he leans over me to undo one wrist, then the other. Last, he cradles my head in his palm to lift the makeshift blindfold out from under me and remove it from my eyes.

We hold eye contact then.

There's eight years and a million words held in the space of that stare. Cradled there.

There's a whole entire universe that lives within the walls of this house and the chambers of our hearts and the buoyant laugh of the human our love made.

And it's there, in that stare.

"I love you," he says.

"I love you too," I reply.

Day 19

Discuss your favorite parts of your wedding day.

(Then, read the next prompt to prepare for tomorrow.)

"Should we watch it first?" I ask Daniel, who is cleaning up the kitchen after breakfast-for-dinner with Violet. There are chunks of banana splattered on the floor, scrambled eggs in the creases of her high chair cover, and syrup all over her fingers—which leave sticky handprints as she cruises under the island. We're going to be in trouble when she starts walking for real.

"Watch what?" he answers, as he disconnects the tray from her chair and brings it to the sink to wash.

"Our wedding video. We could pause it to discuss our favorite parts throughout." The idea of curling up on the couch and watching our younger selves pledge our undying love feels way more fun than another conversation. Not that we've had many of those with the nature of the prompts lately. I certainly haven't minded.

"Oh. Yeah, sure—sounds fun. I'll put Lettie to bed if you want to find it and pull it up. I wouldn't even know where to start with that." He grabs our sweet girl under the arms and hikes her up to sit on his forearm. She looks like a bird perched on a tree, with sticking-up hair to complete the image. Daniel runs his fingers through it and they come back tacky. "I'll give her a quick bath first. Be down in fifteen."

"Use the new lavender soap I put by the tub—it's supposed to help calm her before bedtime."

"Yes, ma'am," he says, and it catches me off-guard. Three weeks ago, he would've been defensive. *I know how to give the baby a bath, Molls.* Today, he's receptive, understanding my request isn't a commentary on his abilities, or presumed incompetence. While I know we've been getting closer physically—how could we not, with everything we've been doing—these moments of emotional understanding are even more profound. We're assuming the best in each other. We're on the same page. Even better, it feels like we're on the same team. It's exactly what I hoped for when we started this experiment.

The relief that this is working is palpable in my body. It's in the way the base of my neck doesn't ache at the end of the day, and my teeth don't wake up clenched. I feel it when Daniel glides a hand along my waist as I'm cooking dinner, and I'm no longer annoyed at the distraction. When I catch his gaze across the table and he smiles, and I smile, and my chest flushes warm with the crinkle of his eyes. It's working.

When I hear his footfall on the stairs, I'm no closer to having our wedding video ready than when he left. I scramble to the drawer in the tv stand and squat, yanking it open as the wood squeaks. Sorting through old DVDs and even older Blu-Rays—none of which we've watched in years—I find our wedding video on its small thumb drive.

"Find it in that mess somehow?" Daniel asks as he places two hands on my shoulders, kneading gently while peeking at the drawer.

"Easy-peasy," I reply with a quiet hum as his fingers work my muscles. "If you get your computer, I'll get the HDMI cord."

He returns with his laptop in hand and two minutes later we're splayed out on the couch, me in one corner and him in the middle, with my legs draped over his lap. He's taken up my feet with his massage hands when I press play.

Pachelbel's Canon in D lilts softly as the title rolls, our names and the date printed in script. After so long, seeing my first name next to my maiden name feels foreign. Daniel digs his thumb along one of my soles.

"I liked having the string quartet," he says, and when I look in his direction, his head is tilted pensively.

"You were adamant that a jazz trio would've been better, if I recall correctly."

"Is this the part where I admit that you were right? Maybe for the reception, but for the ceremony it would've been obnoxious. I should've learned then to listen to you the first time," he replies.

"Your words, not mine," I chuckle in response.

The camera pans to the door at the back of the church, which opens to reveal my mom and grandpa beginning their walk toward the front pew. Mom waves like everyone's there to see her and the first time we watched this video back, I couldn't decide whether to laugh or cringe. I hadn't considered that part of being the bride—everyone gets to see the processional but you.

Next, my grandma and Daniel's grandmothers round into the frame, each carrying a basket of flower petals. When we asked them to be our honorary flower girls, they were absolutely tickled. While two of the three toss the flowers delicately from side to side, one—I'll allow her to remain nameless—uses them to chuck at her family members in the audience. That definitely made me cringe. The bridesmaids are next, each in flowing light blue organza, linked in arms with Daniel's brothers and best friends.

"I really did like those dresses," I say, though not a single one of my friends ever wore hers again, though I swore they would.

"They match your eyes," he says in response, and I'm about to roll mine when I meet his stare and he's earnest. He's not being a smart ass. He means it.

"Alright, Romeo, simmer down," I reply.

Then, with a change of song and increased volume, the doors close and I can feel myself there. I'm taking deep breaths of old must with light from the stained glass warming the back of my neck and my dad's hand resting on mine. "Ready to do this?" he says, and had I said no he would've brought a car around himself to take me home. "Absolutely," I replied instead.

The doors open and everyone stands. The camera pans from me, in a mermaid-cut satin gown with lace on the bust and straps, to Daniel. In his navy suit, he's as handsome as he's ever been. His brother hands him a napkin and he dabs his eyes, but even that can't conceal a megawatt smile.

That's another thing that stings about being the bride—everyone else sees your beloved's reaction to you, but you.

"I was barely keeping it together," he laughs, then switches his attention to rub my other foot.

"If you weren't crying, I would've been concerned."

"Because I cry at movies so often?"

"Because you cry over the horses in the Anheuser-Busch commercials. If I wasn't worth the same treatment as a Superbowl ad, I would've revolted," I reply.

"It was overwhelming, seeing you like that. God, you looked so beautiful."

My dad is kissing my cheek and shaking Daniel's hand now, having given me away (what a bizarre thing, looking back). Then, Daniel and I are face to face, gripping each other's hands for anchor.

"We should've written our own vows," I say, as the officiant walks us through the standard set of promises.

"I don't know—there's something cool about reciting the same words people have been pledging for centuries."

"Do you think we've done right by them?" I ask.

"The more important question is, do you think we've done right by each other? I think we have."

Nodding for a moment to think, I answer, "I think we have, too."

We've been blessed with health, not sickness, and have landed solidly between richer and poorer. We've definitely loved, and we're getting better at cherishing. And these last few weeks, we've done *a lot* of having and holding.

A cry, sharp and incessant, tears through the living room when Daniel and I exchange rings. When we don't rush to get her in three seconds flat, Violet responds with another.

"Hard to believe that day led to all this," he says as I stand. "It was a perfect beginning."

"I think this messy middle is pretty perfect too. Finish this another time?" I ask.

"Any time you want. See ya in bed, wife." The wink he gives is subtle. Flirty. Intentioned

And while it's not our wedding night, I have a feeling tonight will be better.

Day 20

You'd think, after all the filth I've heard and said over the last three-ish weeks, that putting something in writing would be easy.

You'd be wrong.

While Violet babbles in the seat of the grocery cart, I wrack my brain to find something sexy to say. Should I be doing this in the canned veggie aisle? Probably not, but the day's errands can't be skipped on account of needing to draft a slutty SMS.

Daniel started the day easily, texting me immediately after getting into his car (while still in the garage—the door hadn't even opened yet):

> I can't wait to get my hands on you tonight.

My first instinct was to say, "Same!" or give the message a thumbs up, but that's a cop out. I went with the slightly better,

> I can't wait to have your hands on me.

There. I did it.

Violet and I stroll through the dairy aisle where I shiver against the cold. "Let's get you some yogurt," I say to my happy babe, who smiles back. God, I can't wait until she can talk. There's something maddening about narrating the world aloud for your baby's benefit while they can't respond, but I do it anyway, because I read that hearing more words during the first 1000 days of life is associated with better test scores, or something.

Buzz.

My heart rate spikes with the vibration of a text message. Maybe it's Mom, wanting to know if we'll come over for dinner on Sunday.

It's not.

Just my hands, or you want my tongue too?

Suddenly, the chill emanating from the open refrigerator door dissipates. A creeping warmth splashes pink across my neck and chest—I can feel it.

Both. And more than that, too.

I debated adding an eggplant emoji for effect.

Are you feeling shy, baby? You can tell me you want my cock. I know you do.

I slap my phone facedown against the handle of the cart before anyone might see. Violet flaps her hands in intimation, smacking them against the cart. "That's right, Vi," I whisper to her, "We're all done with that for now."

I don't hear anything from Daniel for the next several hours, either because he's waiting for my response or he's tied up in meetings. When my phone buzzes during Violet's second nap—early afternoon—I set down my book and grab it from the ottoman.

You *did* get shy on me. Was that too much?

His ability to prioritize my comfort is one of the best things about him. It's endearing.

No, just been busy with errands and getting Violet down.

It feels strange to follow up that text with something sexy, so I try a different tactic. Leaning forward on the couch, I place my elbows on my knees. Bringing my upper arms to press against the side of my breasts, I create some surprisingly substantial cleavage and practice angling the phone to maximize the impact. The shirt I'm wearing isn't meant for this kind of exposure—it's a V-neck sweater from JCrew I've had forever—but with a tug at the hem, I pull it down just enough to frame my tits beautifully. After no less than fifteen shots I deem unworthy, I take one I like and text it to Daniel before I get sheepish.

Hot DAMN, mama

Fuck

His curse makes me laugh. The giggle tickles up my throat and buoys my confidence so much that I pull the sweater off entirely. Once I've slipped out of my bra straps and let the cups pool around my waist, I look at the camera once more. Maybe these tits aren't as tired as I thought? I throw an arm across myself, taking care to lean forward and scoop them together so they sit nice and high. I angle my forearm down so just a hint of my nipples are showing. For deniability's sake, I pretend they could be shadows. With only five attempts this time, I capture the shot and send it to Daniel.

The fluttering ellipses on the screen stop and start, then stop again. My stomach sinks. What was I thinking? The man is *at work*. I'm not even a year postpartum. Maybe he didn't want to see all of that.

Oh, he did.

He *really* did, because his next message says,

> I'd give anything to lick up your chest right now. How am I supposed to work on this fucking spreadsheet when you're topless and taunting me with your perfect fucking tits?

With no more desire to be coy, and bolstered by the unfettered desire in his words, I reply,

> How about you put your cock between my tits instead of your tongue?

Never once, in our years of marriage or dating before that, have we tried titty fucking. But after the last few days of *exploring*, it sounds fun enough. Plus, I can picture him reading the text at his desk, thrown back in his chair, with one hand rearranging himself in his pants and the other tugging on his hair. He's going to be jumping out of his skin with three more hours to go in the office.

> Would you spit on it for me?

> Yep. And I'd lean down and lick the tip. You'd hit my tongue every time you pushed up. You wouldn't last long.

> You wouldn't either. How wet are you right now? Tell me.

> No wait. Show me.

I'm not about to take a photo of my pussy—a girl has a right to boundaries—but it doesn't stop me from sliding two fingers beneath my panties and dipping them inside the growing pool at my entrance. *Shit.*

Withdrawing them, I place the sticky digits on either side of my nipple and use my left hand to snap a photo. It captures the glistening liquid stringing between my fingers just how I wanted. His reply comes as fast as I send it.

> FUCK, Molly. Fuck me. Are you trying to kill me?

> No, but I AM trying to fuck you later.

> Can you take one more for me? I've got a meeting in five and I need four to deal with this raging semi but I need one more. Lick your fingers for me, baby.

I don't need my years of people pleasing to convince me of his request. My tongue slides flat from my mouth, and I place my index and middle finger to weigh on it. With my camera switched to boomerang (I'm a millennial after all), I hit record and close my lips to suck. When I've licked them clean, I take one more photo of me licking the tip of my finger.

Should I be concerned about hackers finding these some day? Or them ending up on the dark web? It's too late for that; I hit send.

Imagining Daniel writhing, unable to calm himself and trying to will his body to retreat, has me feeling smug. Powerful. Sexy as hell, even with a messy bun and pair of leggings clinging to my body.

> DO NOT text me again, Molls. I'm serious, I can't take it. Don't respond to this next one until you can do so in person.

I nod, waiting for whatever last word he wants to get in. After thirty seconds, the wall of text appears:

When I get home, we're going to get Violet to bed. And then you're MINE, baby. I'm going to lap at your pussy until there's nothing wet left because I've swallowed it all. I'll make sure you're flooded again before I fuck you, and you will be, because you can't help but gush when I pull your nipples into my mouth and tug. You're going to be begging for my cock, Molls.

And after this, today? Making me hard in my office?

I'm going to make it hard for you. Maybe I won't let you come. Maybe I won't let you STOP coming.

When I get home, you better be ready to play.

Day 21

Praise your partner for their effort over the last three weeks.

"I know the prompt says to praise each other, but can we praise the creators of this deck? Should we send them a thank you gift or something?" The vibration of Daniel's chuckle travels all the way to my toes which are inched under his thighs.

"I'm sure they'd appreciate an Amazon review," I say, sitting catty corner to him on the couch. "Do you want to risk that someone sees your review, though? What if they use your quote in social media ads? *'Best sex of my life,' Daniel H., age 32."*

"If that's my legacy, so be it. Print it on my headstone and in my obituary, and bury me with a smile on my face." He lifts his beer in a mock toast before taking a sip.

"It has been good, hasn't it?"

"So fucking good, Molls. All of it. Not just the sex, but also being excited about each other again. Talking through the hard shit. Thinking about the future," he says.

"Fully agree. Thank you for leaning in with me. I didn't have a plan B if you would've scoffed at the idea."

"In that case, you should've put all the sexy cards on my pillow with a post-it note saying NO or SORRY on each one. Really make me feel the pain of what I could've had, you know?"

"I think about that a lot," I reply.

His quirked eyebrow has me backtracking. "Not about a scheme had you said no, but the what ifs. What if I never saw the ad? What if I hadn't been awake in the middle of the night and desperate enough to click *Buy?* What if I'd chickened out instead of asking you to do this with me?" Bile rises in my throat, choking at the words.

"It happened exactly like it was supposed to. But you know what?"

"What?"

"I think we would've found our way back eventually, even without the challenge. Maybe it would've taken longer, or been a bit more painful, but we would've figured it out. I think, at least," he says.

"Maybe, maybe not. I'm glad we don't have to find out."

He sets his bottle on the coffee table and reaches for my feet, bringing them to his lap and warming them with the grasp of his palms.

"I didn't know what to expect when we started this," he says. "I thought it was going to be some sort of woo-woo feelings stuff like love languages."

"There's nothing wrong with love languages!" I interject.

He raises his hands in front of his chest with a laugh. "I know, I know! I'm just saying, I didn't expect this to be fun. I thought it would feel like work, because we had—and still have—a lot of work to do to build the marriage and family we want. But doing these prompts with you has been so much fun. Thank you for encouraging us to do it."

The praise goes down easy, like a cold water on a hot day, satisfying the part of me that loves to be right. "Thank you for doing it with me."

"You really have been incredible. Do you know that?" he asks.

"In bed? Yes. You're welcome," I joke, and his hands are back on my feet, running a tickly finger straight up the sole while I yelp.

"I'm serious. I mean, yes, in bed—holy shit—but also your commitment to this experience. I know you're worn down by the end of the day from Violet and all of your other responsibilities, but each night you've still been all in on whatever the card asks. Watching you fight for us? I want to fight just as hard."

"You have been. Every night, you're more eager than I am to jump into the unknown. You haven't shied away from any of it. Opening up about your dad? I know how hard that was for you, and you were brave—not just for me, but for us. Your vulnerability is a gift, Dan. And we are so lucky to have it. Please keep sharing it."

He blinks and sniffs and shakes his head to fight back the emotion rising in his chest. "Okay, yes, thank you. But can that be enough for tonight? These talking cards are..." he blows through his lips, trilling instead of finishing the thought.

"Knowing this won't be the last conversation, because having these talks is something we do now? Yes, we can be done."

He clears his throat, then says with a grin, "Maybe tomorrow will be another spicy card. I'm digging this every-other-day thing. Both my soul and my dick appreciate the day in between to recover."

"I bet tomorrow's spicy. And we can keep this up, you know, even when the cards are done."

"My soul and my dick are in full agreement with that plan. Sign us up," he says on a laugh, while reaching for my shoulder and pulling me to him, to fit me alongside his body. Our muscles mold by memory, by heart.

"Me too. I want more of this."

"This is the right thing to want more of."

Day 22

Connect outside the bedroom.

Daniel doesn't know that I read the day's card without him. If he did, he'd be privy to my plan to join him in the shower a minute from now. Is it probable that today's prompt meant, "Do something non-sexual together"? Yes. Did we *connect outside the bedroom* in the living room last week? Also yes. Let's just say the card is open to interpretation, and my preferred interpretation is shower sex.

I slip into the bathroom unnoticed; the pounding of the water and whatever tune Daniel's humming cover my footsteps. Next: I head to the closet to shed my uniform (athleisure that says *she's going to the gym* but means *she's no longer interested in hard pants and underwires*). I take inventory of my naked body in the mirror. Stretch marks line my stomach and the side of my hips. There's a softness now where my collarbone used to show and where my abs were once defined.

That's what I notice, but it's not what I *see*. Tonight, I see a woman sculpted out of marble, with a body so worthy of worship, it's captured forever in stone. I'm Venus de Milo, and my cellulite is chisel marks from a master artist.

I see myself through Daniel's eyes—those hungry, heavy pools that linger on the parts of me I spent so long covering.

For the first time, I see myself clearly, as a strong woman with a body that can create new life and bring another to his knees. I'm at home in my body; I'm embodied.

I glide from the closet to the shower door, swinging it open with a bit too much force and closing it gently on account of the glass.

"Baby?" Daniel says, with his back and enviable ass toward me and his face in the water's stream.

"Figured you wouldn't mind company," I reply, stepping behind him and wrapping my arms around his middle. My head finds its home in the notch between his shoulder blades.

"Never, come here." He spins until we're chest to chest and I'm pressed against his warm, wet skin. "What's the occasion?"

While yes, it's been awhile since we've showered together, does a wife need a reason to get sudsy with her spouse?

"The day's card," I reply. "We're supposed to *connect outside the bedroom*. As far as I'm concerned, the bathroom counts."

"Definitely counts."

With a thumb on my chin and his fingers gripping my ass, he brings his mouth to mine. Slow, searching kisses with gentle swipes of his tongue until I can feel his erection growing against me. Then it's deeper kisses and roaming hands, skin slipping against skin as we feel and tug, nip and tease until my nipples are pebbled and the wetness between my legs is making me dirty, not clean.

"How 'bout I sit?" he says, backing himself to the bench that lines the shower's wall. With a sweep of his hand, shampoo bottles and body wash pumps fall to the floor. A chorus echoes through the space as raindrops hit the half-empty bottles, each with their own tone as water slaps the plastic in rhythm. It's the sort of noise that would bother me if I wasn't entirely focused on straddling Daniel's lap.

With spread legs and a gaze so heated it makes me shiver, he brings me on top of him. My pussy rests on his cock until I lift up on my knees. I reach between us and grip him at the base, sliding him between my lips to tease both of us, tip to clit, before bringing him to my entrance. With unwavering eye contact, I take him inch by inch until we're both fully seated—him inside me and my ass on the top of his thighs. In this position, at this angle, his length takes up every millimeter of space, stuffing me full. I feel him at my cervix, at my entrance, pushing against my walls. He's everywhere and I can barely breathe.

"God, you feel so good, baby," he says with fingertips in the flesh of my hips. He's still, I'm still, and the pressure of him between my legs has me aching for movement, fearful it will dissipate. I wrap my arms around his neck, lean my forehead on his shoulder and grind against him. My moan echoes in the steam and hovers.

"*You* feel so good," I whimper.

I set a rhythm: rocking, grinding, sometimes leaning too far forward so he almost slips out before slamming back down. Stars puncture the black behind my eyes as he groans, brings his hands to my hair, sucks at my neck to leave a bruise. It's so much and it's still not enough.

I need more of his touch. I need stimulation beyond the glorious, relentless pounding at my g-spot. To grant him access to my chest, my clit, I bring my hands to my heels. Here, I am wide open for the taking. Daniel drops his eyes to watch as he disappears into my body, in and out and back again. He tilts a hand to rub his thumb against the most sensitive part of me, up and down and then in circles, never taking his eyes off my pussy and the way I welcome him into my body.

It builds quickly, pleasure and pressure low in my belly. My legs begin to tremble with it, my fingers losing purchase on my slippery feet. He keeps one hand at my clit and wraps a strong arm around my waist, holding me up.

"Look at me, Molls," he says while we're eye to eye and my body rocks with need, without conscious thought. "Look at me when you come."

"Now? Please, tell me I can come now?" I ask on a choked breath.

"Yes, come for me, baby."

And I do, with a soft body and sparks dancing on my skin and my eyes locked on his as he follows.

"We should probably clean you up," he says, after a languid, lingering moment with our foreheads pressed together and heavy exhales between us.

Pointing to the bottles on the floor as I climb off his lap, I say, "That *is* what the shower's for," and he rolls his eyes like he's sick of me (endearing).

With a warm washcloth in hand, he sweeps between my legs to clear what he can of his release. Then, with a rinse and a fresh squirt of soap, he brings it to my back. In the quiet and steam, he serves me, honors me, loves me from my head to my toes. With gentle strokes, he roughs away the dead and I welcome the new.

I feel new, and it feels so good.

Day 23

Bake something together.

Making chocolate chip cookies for Violet to "leave out for Santa" is one of the sweetest ideas Daniel's had—literally and figuratively. Of course, she's too young to understand any of it, and we probably won't let her eat one, but I'm swooning at the birth of a new family tradition. I can see years-worth of family photos, Violet growing from a round baby to a bow-legged toddler to a gap-toothed girl, sitting next to a plate of half-eaten cookies on Christmas morning. I can see years-worth of Daniel and me, progressively grayer and more wrinkled, laughing and playfully arguing about forgetting to soften the butter.

"Do you think this baking powder is still good?" he asks, bringing the box to his nose for a sniff.

"It doesn't really spoil," I say as I grab the box from his hand, chuckling. "If it's bad, the cookies will turn out flat."

"So is that a yes or a no on whether it's good?"

"I've got another box—it's on the top shelf behind the flour. Grab both, the chocolate chips, and the vanilla."

He ambles to the pantry and I give myself a second to watch his rear as he does. It's cliche, but the gray sweatpants effect is real. He looks good.

Tearing myself from his ass, I collect the butter and eggs, and grab the sugar, brown sugar, and salt. We both approach the counter with an armful of baking supplies.

"Wet or dry?" I ask, while wondering if he knows what I'm asking.

"Dry for me. I always want you wet," he answers with a wink, and desire drips like molasses, sticky down my spine.

Cookies, Molly, I remind myself. *Don't get distracted.*

With a cleared throat, I shove the brown sugar and salt his way.

"For you to mix," I reply, and it's a miracle I don't smack his ass with a spatula while I'm at it.

"Yes, ma'am," he says with a smirk.

We peer at the small index card with my mother's handwriting, our foreheads almost touching from opposite sides of the island. We scour the list for our ingredients and their volumes, even while a brown, ragged splash—a drop of a vanilla from years ago—obscures part of it. The card is smudged, worn around the edges. There's a metaphor there, I'm sure, about love and worth and effort.

"How many cookies are you eating tonight?" Daniel asks as I roll an egg, smooth and cold, between my palms.

"At least two. Maybe three. You?"

He tilts his head and squints one eye, in an expression so familiar I could draw it by memory. *Thinking Face*, I'd title it. "Probably five. I was going to say three, but then I thought—we're being vulnerable these days. Why lie?"

"A cookie confession. I love it," I reply, before leaning forward and kissing his lips. Just a peck to tide me over.

With the butter appropriately soft, it's time to cream the sugar. I turn on the hand mixer while Daniel portions out half and quarter teaspoons of fresh baking powder and salt. "Pass me the vanilla?" I ask when the butter is whippy and more white than yellow. He palms it, walks to my side of the island, and positions himself behind me.

"How much?" he asks, with his hands on the edge of the counter, bracketing me in. I lean my head against the solid weight of his arm and the kiss he presses to my neck, breathy and warm, skips straight to my heart.

"Two teaspoons." I lift the small silver spoon, but rather than take it from me, he turns my hand level, opens the vanilla and pours it into the hollow.

"There's one," he says, twisting my wrist to let the liquid spill into my bowl. Repeating the process again, he says, "There's two."

It hits like a gasp, the nostalgia already seeping around the corners of the memory we're making. Being wrapped in his arms with sugar under my fingernails and the scent of vanilla blooming in my nose, this is a moment I'll look back on with fondness. When I'm eighty-five and thinking back on my life, *this* is what I'll come back to.

A contented hum leaves my throat as I soak it in, to catalog it.

The oven dings to announce it's done preheating. Daniel takes one more second to nuzzle into my neck, and I relish the scratch of his stubble against my skin, the contrast to the softness of his cheek. "Back to work," he says as he moves toward his side of the counter, though he lets his hand linger on my lower back until he can no longer reach.

I crack the eggs and mix, then grab his bowl. I add the dry ingredients a little at a time, folding them in until they join the mass of dough. Every time I add more, what's in the bowl evolves—a little drier, lighter in color, a firmer texture. There's a metaphor here too, about trusting the process and allowing yourself to be changed.

"Got the chips?" I ask when I have a ball of dough that smells divine and is moldable under my fingers.

"The recipe says one cup of chips for every cup of flour, but I'm doing a cup and a half and I won't be dissuaded."

"Agreed—an excellent use of free will," I reply with a soft smile, and watch as the morsels cascade into the bowl, slowly at first and then en masse. I mix them in by hand, having learned from my mom not to *overwork the dough.*

Then we spoon them and roll balls before flattening them with our fingertips on the greased tray. When all is said and done, we have twenty four cookies. Five for Daniel, three for me, two for Santa and fourteen to eat on Christmas Day when we're hungry at 8 p.m. on account of 3 p.m. dinner at my parents' house.

Is there anything better than the smell of fresh cookies? Maybe the soft snores of a sleeping baby on the monitor, a dusting of snow on the trees, and the eager hands of a handsome man pulling me to the couch while they bake.

"This might be my favorite prompt yet," I say as I slip under Daniel's arm and pull my feet underneath me.

"Better than yesterday?" he replies. "Because yesterday was pretty incredible."

"I'm starting to think each day is my new favorite. It just keeps getting better."

"Tomorrow? Even better yet," he replies.

Day 24

Write a list of 10 prompts each to complete in the future.

S hards of wrapping paper, shiny and half-torn, cover the living room floor and stick to my thighs whenever I change positions. How is it that scissors and scotch tape disappear when it's time to wrap gifts, when you know you have multiples of each somewhere in the house? It leaves Daniel and I stealing them back and forth as we scramble to wrap Violet's presents before the big reveal in the morning.

"You know this is dumb, right?" I say to him as I fold a neat crease and tape it on the side of a brand-new picture book. "Vi is going to care more about crumpling the paper and playing with the boxes than she is the toys. We could've saved so much time and money. Wrapping paper, cardboard, and a fake tv remote, and she would've been thrilled."

He tosses a balled-up wad of paper over my head to the trash pile. "But isn't this part of the fun? *I'm* having fun."

"*I'm* getting paper cuts," I reply, a chuckle tumbling from my lips.

"Want to take a break for the last card?" he asks, stopping his work with a cardboard tube in one hand a pair of scissors open in the other.

"I've been avoiding thinking about it. I'm nervous, almost. What if we wrap up the experiment and the magic leaves? I don't want to stop feeling like this."

"Then we'll start the whole thing over. Amorous Advent can become…" he thinks for a minute before a devious smile graces his face. "Juicy January and Flirtatious February."

"Oh my god, you did not just say *Juicy January*." I accompany the reply with a gag, and his lips rise further, the apples of his cheeks on full display.

"You know what I mean!" he says. "We can keep this thing going. That's what we decided, right? We'll keep doing this."

With a quick dart into the kitchen, Daniel returns with the deck. It's not the nice, smooth rectangle it was twenty-four days ago—some cards are bent, others stick out haphazardly.

It's the living embodiment of our effort, imperfect but complete.

"Yessss," he says as he reads the day's prompt. "Grab a scrap of paper. We're coming up with our own ideas."

I take the card from him and my eyes linger on the words. I guess it really is up to us now.

He finds the pens buried under a stack of to-and-from labels and hands one to me. Armed with a very jolly and not-so-wrinkled piece of reindeer paper with white on the back, I start to draft my list. The words flow quickly, much more fluidly than I expect. With each new idea, excitement tightens against my ribs:

1. Go to a bar and do trivia

2. Discuss ways to hold each other accountable to our goals

3. Visit an adult shop together and buy each other something

4. Watch a re-run of How I Met Your Mother

5. Give each other massages (do a better job this time, no fighting)

6. Have sex somewhere risky

7. Build the back patio (this will take more than a night, I know)

8. I blindfold and tie you up

9. Wax play?

10. Make Violet's first birthday cake together

The list feels exactly right. It's emotional, nostalgic, sexy, and fun. I'd propose starting on it tomorrow if tomorrow wasn't Christmas. I glance at Daniel and he's got on his thinking face again, this time with the pen tucked between his teeth in between bursts of writing.

"Can't think of anything?" I tease.

"Nah, I'm trying to narrow it down. Creating an A list and a B list. We can use the other one for Mesmerizing March."

My eye roll is slow and dramatic. "You're ridiculous," I say.

"You love me," he counters.

"I do. Please, can we switch?" I fold my list in half and hold it between my fingers like I'm offering money for drugs or something similarly illicit. He offers his paper freely. His handwriting, neat and familiar, spells out the following:

1. Blow job in my office, after hours

2. Share the best and worst things that happened that day

3. Recreate our first date

4. I restrain your hands AND feet and have my way with you

5. Finish watching our wedding video

6. Role play

7. Bring Violet to see fireworks

8. Organize the hall closet to create a dedicated space for my golf bag

9. Talk about our goals for the next year

10. Give you a five orgasm night

"Coming five times feels a bit ambitious," I say to Daniel as I hand his list back. "But I'm *very* happy to try."

"We'll get you there, baby, one way or another," he replies with a wink. "But why does wax play have a question mark? If you're in, I'm in. I'll buy some sex-safe candles tomorrow, Christmas or not, if that's what you want."

"I wasn't sure if it'd be too weird for you. Didn't want you to feel pressured to do something you're not into."

"What I'm into is *you*. Whatever you want, I'm open to try."

"Same." Then I backtrack and add, "Well, mostly. How about we both get veto power?"

"Always. So when should we start?"

"Want to kick it off in the new year? We have lots of family time this week anyway, then we can go out on New Year's Eve, have fun, and then buckle down for these new prompts on day one. Make a nightly connect our New Year's resolution."

"Hell yes. I can't wait."

"I can't wait to never stop."

Epilogue

Want to read how Molly and Daniel spend New Year's Eve?

Visit www.mallorythomas.com to download the bonus epilogue. It's fun and spicy, promise!

Acknowledgments

I wrote *Untangled* because I was desperate to remember that I knew how to write. I needed to remind myself that I could craft beautiful lines and swoony moments and spice that makes me sweat. It's the story of:

- Reclaiming the fun in my writing

- Strengthening my instincts after they'd been worn down

- Confronting my lingering tension with explicit, open-door romance as someone who grew up in the early 2000s evangelical church under purity culture

Additionally, I work with new parents for my day job, and *Untangled* is the story of unspoken numbers of new mothers who feel restless in their marriages and unrecognizable, even to themselves.

I wrote this book without input from my agents (sorry Wendy and Callie!) and published it with a self-designed cover. As such, my acknowledgements look a bit different than usual.

To my husband, who never questions my wild ideas, who takes the kids when I need time to write, who models what it looks like to self-reflect and apologize. Fourteen years of marriage and two kids later, and we're better than ever. I love you!

To Courtney Corlew, who inspired me with her own holiday novella quick-turn project, and whose Patreon templates will make up 100% percent of my marketing effort in the month of December.

To the romance author community, which always steps up to answer questions, offer support, lend a hand or point to a needed resource. This industry would be too hard to deal with if it weren't for the people mucking through the trenches with me.

To my sisters, sisters-in-law, mom and mother-in-law, and (God forbid) my dad and father-in-law: please pretend you didn't read this one. Never speak of this with me. Thank you.

To the romance reader community, you're the reason the magic exists. You take chances, spend your hard-earned dollars, shout our books from the social media rooftops and champion us. Thank you for reading. You are the backbone of our art.

If you liked *Untangled*, please leave a review on Goodreads and Amazon, even if you didn't purchase from there. It's the best way you can support an author, and I can't overemphasize how much we want to hug you when you do.

I'd love for you to check out my romance debut, *Somewhere Along The Line* (out now, more story and less spice but the same blush-worthy style) and please add my traditional debut, *Double Standard* (out July 28th, 2026) to your Goodreads shelf!

Thank you for supporting my work. Love ya, mean it.
Mallory

About the Author

Mallory Thomas is a writer and reader of soft love stories that make you swoon, squeal, and blush. When she's not writing, she can be found picking up after her two kids, joking with her handsome husband, and planning trips to the beach. She's also a baby formula expert and content creator. She lives with her family in Nashville, TN.